The making of may

Gwyneth Rees is half Welsh and half English and grew up in Scotland. She went to Glasgow University and qualified as a doctor in 1990. She is a child and adolescent psychiatrist, but has now stopped practising so she can write full-time. Gwyneth is the author of the bestselling Fairies series – which includes *Fairy Dust, Fairy Treasure, Fairy Dreams* and *Fairy Gold* – as well as *Mermaid Magic, Cosmo and the Magic Sneeze* and *Cosmo and the Great Witch Escape*. For older readers she has written *My Mum's from Planet Pluto, The Mum Hunt,* which won the Younger Novel category of the Red House Children's Book Award 2004, and its sequel, *The Mum Detective.* She lives in London with her two cats.

Gwyneth Rees

The Making of May

MACMILLAN CHILDREN'S BOOKS

First published 2006 by Macmillan Children's Books

This edition published 2007 by Macmillan Children's Books
a division of Macmillan Publishers Limited
20 New Wharf Road, London N1 9RR
Basingstoke and Oxford
www.panmacmillan.com

Associated companies throughout the world

ISBN: 978-0-330-43732-5

1 3 5 7 9 8 6 4 2

A CIP catalogue record for this book is available from
the British Library.

Typeset by Intype Libra Ltd
Printed and bound in Great Britain by Mackays of Chatham plc, Kent

For Alice May Burden
— friend, first publicist and wicked brainstormer!

And with thanks to my brilliant editor, Sarah Davies

❋ 1 ❋

There are lots of orphans who appear in books. There's Oliver Twist, Jane Eyre, David Copperfield, Pollyanna and even Bambi – but my favourite orphan in a book is definitely Mary Lennox in *The Secret Garden*. In case you've never heard of it, *The Secret Garden* is a book that was written nearly a hundred years ago about a girl who's an orphan, who goes to live in a gigantic old house, where she finds a walled garden that nobody has been inside for ten years and which she sort of brings back to life again. The thing is that she's ten years old too and *she's* never been cared about until she comes to live in the house with the garden, so the garden and Mary sort of become friends.

I like Mary because she's not too sweet and she's not too pretty, which makes her more like a real person – more like me, in fact. And we've even got the same name. I'm called Mary too – only nobody ever calls me that. They all call me May for short.

On the day *this* book starts, I hadn't read *The Secret Garden* yet, but I had already watched the video ten times. The Mary in the film looks a bit like me. She's quite pale with skinny arms and legs and dirty-blonde straight hair that sits on her shoulders. And she's got a nice face when she smiles but a really scowly one when she doesn't get her own way.

I had just switched the video to PLAY and had settled down on the sofa to watch it again when my big brother, Ben, walked into the room. I didn't look up because my imagination had already been captured by the opening of the film. They play this beautiful haunting music and show pictures of the secret garden and then you see the grand house with a horse and carriage outside so you know it's set in olden times. I know it's an oboe that's playing the music because at the end, when the credits come up, it tells you the name of the oboe soloist. I think maybe I'd like to learn to play the oboe one day if it can sound as beautiful as that. I've got a recorder but it's kind of screechy – or maybe that's just the way I play it.

'How about we go to the park or something?' Ben said. Ben thought I stayed indoors too much. 'The sun's shining outside. Why do you want to be sitting in here with the curtains drawn?'

He went to pull them back and I screeched at him, 'It's too bright to see the telly if you do that.' The television faced the window and when it was really sunny, you couldn't see anything at all on the screen.

Ben doesn't like it when I screech, so he left the curtains alone. He was still standing looking at me though. In *The Secret Garden*, Mary was screeching at her ayah to go away. An ayah is a sort of nanny in India, which is where Mary lives at the start of the story.

'She makes even more noise than you do,' Ben joked, after watching it with me for a few minutes.

Mary was now screeching at a soldier who had come to tell her that everyone she knew – including her parents – had just died of cholera.

'Just go away. You're spoiling it,' I told Ben crossly.

'Well, OK, but when Lou comes back I think we should all go out somewhere.'

Louise is my big sister. Lou and Ben are a lot older than me – she's twenty-two and he's twenty-six. They're only my half-brother and sister really because I've got a different father to them. They know their dad though they don't see him much – whereas I've never even met mine. I'm eleven and I've lived with them since I was four because – just like Mary Lennox – I haven't got any parents either. Lou and Ben had always looked after me together, though since I'd got older I reckoned I was pretty much able to take care of myself. Ben worked whenever he could during the day, doing odd jobs for people, and Lou worked in the evenings as a waitress.

It was Saturday morning and Lou was due back from the supermarket at any minute. I knew she would turn off the TV just like that if she wanted me to stop watching it when she came in. She never cared how much I screeched. Sometimes she screeched back, and Ben hated that because he said the walls were really thin in the council flats where we lived and we'd have the neighbours coming round if we weren't careful. Ben worries a lot about what other people think – too much, Lou says.

I paused the videotape as soon as I heard the front door slamming and Lou yelling out that she was back. I'd got to the bit where Mary first meets the gardener and he introduces her to the robin who lives in the secret garden. I really like that bit in the

3

story and I didn't want Lou spoiling it. My sister swore as she tripped over the loose bit of carpet in the hall – we were meant to be saving up for a new one but so far we weren't doing very well.

'Is Greg here yet?' she called out as she went straight to the kitchen with the shopping.

Greg was her boyfriend – her first ever serious one – and I didn't like him, chiefly because he was always wanting to see Lou on her own, which meant she spent most of the weekend seeing him instead of us. She even stayed the night at his place sometimes. She'd met him at the restaurant where she worked and they'd been going out for six months now. He was going off travelling very soon though, so he wouldn't be around much longer, thank goodness.

'No,' Ben answered as Lou came into the living room. 'You expecting him?'

'*Why* can't he hurry up and leave the country like he keeps *saying* he's going to do?' I grunted.

'He will,' Lou said. 'In a couple of weeks. The thing is . . .' Her voice dried up and she came over to sit on the sofa beside me. 'Sit down a minute, will you, Ben? I've got something important to tell you both.' Her voice sounded a bit funny. She frowned as she pushed her hair out of her eyes. Lou has got blonde hair too, only it's lighter than mine because she colours it. She's also got exactly the same colour eyes as me – light brown with green flecks in them.

I knew it was bad news when I saw how nervous she looked. Lou isn't a nervous person normally. Lou is always talking or laughing or crying or shouting at you, but she hardly ever goes all anxious and quiet like she had gone now.

'Well . . . ?' Ben, who can't stand it when Lou makes

4

a big drama out of things, was starting to look like he could stand it even less when she was all anxious and quiet. 'For God's sake . . . What *is* it?'

'Greg phoned me on my mobile while I was at the shops. He's been asking me to go travelling with him and . . . and I've just said yes.'

'*What?*' I was confused. 'Go travelling *where?*'

'Well . . . to start with we're going to India but—'

'*India?*' I was about to tell her that she couldn't go there because of the cholera, but then I remembered that wasn't actually real. Though, for all I knew, they might still have cholera in India in real life too.

Ben didn't say anything. He looked at my sister as if he'd just had his tongue forcibly stuffed down the back of his throat.

Lou was looking at me, and I got the feeling she was avoiding looking at my brother. 'Yes, and then we're going to Australia for a bit because Greg's got family there. I'll only be gone for a year altogether, May.' (Like I said before, even though my proper name is Mary, I've always been called May. My mother was the only one in our family who liked the name Mary, so after she died there was nobody left who called me that. I'd always thought the name May was much cooler and that Mary was really old-fashioned – until I'd started watching *The Secret Garden*. Now I quite liked the name Mary too.)

'A whole *year!*' I couldn't believe I was hearing this.

'It's a perfectly normal thing to do. Lots of people my age take a year out to go travelling. If Ben wasn't here it would be different.' She looked at my brother then, a little guiltily.

'Good old Ben,' my brother replied drily.

Lou went red then. 'Well, *you're* her guardian.'

5

'I know that.'

I looked from one face to the other, starting to resent the way they were talking about me. Like I was a burden.

I scowled. It wasn't as if I didn't know they'd both be free to do whatever they wanted if it wasn't for me.

I stood up. 'Go away if you want! I don't care.' And I stormed out of the room into the bedroom I shared with Lou and slammed the door.

They weren't paying much attention to me though. As I left Ben said sarcastically, 'And you'd be taking a year out of *what*, exactly?' And then they started to argue.

A minute or so later, in among the raised voices coming from the other room, there was a loud rapping on the front door. Our doorbell needed a new battery, but Ben never wanted to spend money on things that weren't essentials. I heard Louise go and open the door and say something in a low voice to Greg. She didn't invite him inside. I knew if she was going out with him today, she'd need to come into the room to get her things so I sat stiffly on my bed, waiting for her.

Maybe she wouldn't really go. Maybe it was just an idea that sounded nice, but when it came to it she'd stay here with us.

But when she came into the room I could see by her face that she was determined about this. In fact, she had a look on her face as if she had already left us behind.

'Lou, you haven't got any money to go on holiday,' I pointed out. The three of us hadn't had a proper holiday for as long as I could remember because we never had any spare cash.

'This isn't a holiday – it's travelling,' she replied. 'I'll get work. We'll be staying with Greg's aunt and uncle in Australia for a while – Greg reckons we can get work in bars and stuff. And he's paying for my ticket to start with.'

Greg had bought her quite a few things since they'd started going out – meals in restaurants, tickets for the cinema, a weekend away in Brighton. Once he had bought her a new pair of boots that she had seen in a sale and fallen in love with. Ben and Lou had had a row that day because Greg had offered to buy me a pair of boots in the sale too. Apparently, they had seen these cute little red ones that they thought would really suit me, but Ben had argued that we weren't so hard up that we needed to accept other people's charity.

Lou came and sat beside me on my bed. 'Please don't be angry. This is a big chance for me. I'm really excited about it.'

'Really excited about leaving *us*, you mean,' I said crossly. '*Thanks!*'

'Oh, May, you know I'll really miss you.' Lou reached out to touch my arm.

'Do you *love* Greg?' I demanded, pulling my arm away.

Lou smiled. 'I've never felt this way about a guy before, if that's what you're asking.'

'Do you love *him* more than you love *us*?' I knew it was a babyish question but I didn't care.

She was frowning now. 'Listen, May . . . you and me and Ben have all got much closer to each other than we would've done if Mum hadn't died. And I'm really glad we've stayed together and been a family all this time. But now I want to leave home like normal people my age do, OK?'

I scowled. I really didn't like what she was saying to me. 'But what if *Ben* wants to leave home too?' I said stroppily. 'What if *he* decides to go off travelling as well?' Just saying those words made me feel sick. Imagine if I didn't have Louise *or* Ben here to look after me . . .

'Don't be silly! Ben *is* home as far as you're concerned. Until you're grown up, anyway. He might as well be your dad.'

I nodded, because it was true that Ben was more like a dad than a big brother to me. 'And you're like my mum,' I added.

But she shook her head then. 'No – that's the whole point! That's what I'm trying to say!' She sighed. 'Listen . . . me and Ben and you . . . we're a bit like a mum and a dad and a kid half the time, aren't we? But that's not really what we are, May, and I don't want it to be like that any more. Because one day I want to have a family with someone who's not my brother . . .' She flushed. '. . . maybe even with Greg, if it works out. Can you understand that?'

I looked at her, finding myself feeling stuff that scared me. I felt like I could feel all her hopes for the future inside *me* all of a sudden and I could feel how much she wanted things to turn out right with Greg. But for things to work with Greg, she had to leave *us*.

'I don't know,' I mumbled.

'Listen, we'll talk some more later. I've got to go now or we'll be late for the doctor's. Greg's got me an appointment to get some travel vaccinations.'

So she wouldn't be dying of cholera then. That was something.

'Try and understand, May,' she said as she stood up to go. 'Life hasn't been that easy, so far, has it? I just want to do something *fun*.'

✱ 2 ✱

Ben came into my room after Lou and Greg had gone out, and I could tell he was in a strange mood.

'Come on. We're getting away from here for the day. We're going to the seaside.'

'I'd rather just watch the rest of my video,' I told him.

'Just do as you're told for once, OK?'

I sulked the whole way to the train station. I really wanted to be inside watching my video, not outside with no way of escaping all the upsetting thoughts that were whirling round in my brain. I couldn't believe that my sister was leaving us. Louise was the person I had always thought understood me best of all. She was the one who had bought me the videotape of *The Secret Garden* in the first place. She'd discovered it in a charity shop and we'd watched it together the same day, curled up on the sofa with a packet of chocolate biscuits.

I couldn't imagine not seeing my sister for a whole year. I didn't think I could actually bear to be separated from her for that long. OK, so I was still going to have Ben, but he just didn't like talking about feelings – his or anybody else's – the way Lou did, which meant that when I was worried about stuff, Lou tended to be the person I went to.

I dragged my feet as I walked along the road, feeling really sorry for myself. I especially felt sorry that I was an orphan, because if I wasn't – and Lou was my mum instead of just my big sister – she wouldn't be leaving me, would she?

Sometimes, when you're feeling really sad and you don't know what to do, it really helps just to know that someone else is in the same situation as you. The trouble is, nobody else I know is an orphan. I'm not saying that nobody else in the whole world is – obviously lots of children are – but the thing is, I don't know any of them. So the nearest thing I had right then to a friend who knew how I felt was Mary Lennox in *The Secret Garden*.

Up until today, I'd always thought I was better off than Mary Lennox, because she didn't have *anyone* who'd ever loved her – even before her parents died they didn't care about her – whereas I had Lou and Ben. But now that Lou was leaving me, I almost wished that, just like Mary at the start of *The Secret Garden*, I didn't have anyone or anything important in *my* life either. At least that way you'd never have anyone or anything important to lose. Except that it must be pretty horrible not caring about anyone or having anyone who cares about you.

As I trudged along the road beside my brother I started to think how that's what *The Secret Garden* is all about really. I mean, it's about Mary finding the garden and bringing it back to life and everything, but it's also about how Mary learns to care about things for the first time there. She starts to care more and more about the garden itself, and at the same time she's making friends with the robin and the old gardener and a boy who knows all about growing things. And as the garden gradually comes back to life again, Mary sort of comes alive inside too.

If Louise had been with me, I'd have told her what I was thinking, but since she wasn't, I kept quiet. I thought Ben might not understand and, in any case, I got the feeling that he wasn't in a mood for talking.

When we arrived at the station, my brother swore when he saw the queue at the ticket office.

I'd always hated our local train station. There was graffiti on everything – even worse than on the outside of our flats – and if someone had been sick on the platform, it stayed there for ages because no one ever bothered to clean it up. You only had to go one short stop on the train to get to the town centre where all the shops were, but I still always preferred to get the bus.

We stood waiting impatiently as the person at the front of the queue started asking lots of questions.

'We're not going to make it,' I said when we heard the announcement that our train was arriving. Everyone else in the queue was starting to complain loudly too – but the person at the front still wasn't hurrying.

Ben frowned. 'It's a whole hour to wait if we miss this one,' he said. And he left the queue and beckoned me to follow him up the steps to the platform.

'What about our tickets?' I asked, when I'd caught up with him at the top of the stairs.

'They don't deserve our money if that's their idea of providing a service,' he grunted. 'Don't worry –

12

they hardly ever check your ticket on the train. I've done this before. It's easy.'

That's when I remembered something Lou had said once when she and Ben were having an argument. He had been criticizing her about something and she had yelled back, 'Well, it's not like you're so perfect either. At least I haven't been fined for fare-dodging!' When I'd asked her about it afterwards she'd told me that Ben had been caught fare-dodging on the train when he was fourteen. He'd been doing it a lot with a mate in the year after their father left.

'Lou said you got caught when you did it before,' I said, staying close to him as we got to the platform where quite a lot of people were boarding the train.

'Yeah – one time I was unlucky,' he admitted, sounding bitter as he added, 'that was back in the carefree days of my youth – before I transformed into Mr No-Life-of-His-Own-But-Totally-Ultra-Responsible.' He was heading along the platform away from the main crowd of people, holding me tightly by the arm. Ben always likes to keep hold of me when we're in busy places, even though I keep telling him I'm not going to get lost.

I just stared at him. He was acting really weird and I was starting to feel scared. 'Ben, what if we get caught?'

'We won't!' Ben said. 'Come on.' He had stopped at a carriage towards the end of the train and now he was pressing the button that opened the door.

Reluctantly I followed him inside. The carriage we had chosen wasn't very full. We stopped at the first set of four empty seats with a table that we came to. Since we both like facing the way the train's going,

Ben waited for me to go in first to get the window seat. But today I didn't want the window seat. I wanted to sit in the aisle so I could keep a lookout for any ticket inspectors.

'*You* sit by the window,' I told him.

Once we'd settled into our seats and the train had set off, I started to look around at the other passengers. There were a few people seated further down the carriage, but the person I could see best was the man sitting on his own just across the aisle from me. Since he was concentrating on reading his newspaper he was quite easy to stare at. I thought he looked about the same age as Ben and Louise's father, who's in his mid-fifties. (Ben hasn't seen his dad in ages because they don't get along, but I'd seen him last year when he'd come to the flat to visit Lou.) The man was clean-shaven, with short greying hair, balding at the front, and a stern face. He was dressed in a smart suit and his overcoat was folded up neatly beside the briefcase that was sitting on the empty seat beside him. On the table in front of him was a large white cake box tied with string. It was sliding around a bit with the movement of the train and he kept putting out his hand to steady it. He was obviously worried that it would slide right off the table because, after a particularly bumpy bit of track, he got up, carefully lifted the cake box with both hands and placed it on the empty seat opposite him.

I turned to Ben, meaning to ask him what he thought about Louise going off travelling. So far we hadn't talked about it at all and I figured that, as he was trapped in the window seat next to me, he wouldn't be able to get out of answering my questions now. But

Ben's eyes were shut and when I asked him if he was asleep he didn't reply.

We stopped at the main station in town then and a lot more people got on. I glanced across the aisle at the man with the cake and saw that his eyes were closed now too.

As we started moving again Ben opened his eyes and said he needed to use the toilet, so I had to get up to let him out. He hadn't been gone long when the doors between our carriage and the next opened and two middle-aged ladies came in, carrying loads of shopping bags. The first lady wasn't looking where she was going because she was talking to her friend who was behind her. She dumped her bags down on the seat facing mine and that's when I realized that the seats they were actually going to sit in were the two on the other side of the aisle – opposite the man – and that they hadn't seen the cake.

I yelled out, 'DON'T SIT DOWN!' at the top of my voice.

I was just in time. I pointed at the cake box, and the woman quickly put out a hand to steady herself on the back of the seat instead of sitting on it.

The man woke up with a start. 'I'm so sorry! Here . . . Let me move that for you!'

But the two ladies had spotted some more empty seats and were already moving on down the train, bashing everyone with their shopping bags as they went.

I watched as the man gently lifted his precious cake box and put it back on to the table.

'You should put your newspaper underneath it,' I advised him. 'Then it won't slip around as much.'

He smiled at me then, which made him look a lot

friendlier. 'Quite a practical young lady, aren't you?' he said lightly, as he unfolded his paper and actually did as I'd suggested. (I was pleasantly surprised since my brother and sister rarely took any notice of me when I suggested solutions to *their* problems.) 'Thanks for your timely intervention just then, by the way,' he added. 'Otherwise I'm afraid this splendid cake would be somewhat flatter than it is now.'

'And it would have that lady's bum marks in it,' I pointed out.

He smiled but put his finger to his lips to warn me that the lady in question might be sitting near enough to hear us. He had friendly little wrinkles that appeared around his eyes when he smiled – like cats' whiskers.

'Is there a really *special* cake inside your box then?' I asked.

'Would you like me to show you?'

I nodded eagerly, getting out of my seat and standing over him as he untied the string around the box. The train was swaying a bit and I had to hold on to the edge of his table to steady myself.

Ben came back then and wanted to know what I was doing. He always gets jumpy if he thinks I'm talking to strangers. He reckons I'm far too trusting of people I don't know and ever since I was little he's worried that some stranger is going to try and abduct me by promising to buy me sweets, or show me some really cute kittens, or do whatever it is that strangers do to make you go off with them.

'It's OK, Ben,' I told him. 'He's just showing me his special cake.'

The man added quickly, 'It's a birthday cake for my son, which the young lady here . . .' He turned to me apologetically. 'Sorry . . . I haven't asked your name . . .'

'Mary,' I told him. For some reason I wanted him to know my full name, not the shortened version.

'. . . which *Mary* here,' he continued, 'has very gallantly just saved from being sat on!'

As I started to explain to Ben exactly what had happened, the man opened the white cardboard lid to reveal the most amazing cake I had ever seen. It was shaped like a red aeroplane and looked as if it was completely edible except for the wings – they were red and shiny as if they belonged on a real model plane.

'Wow!' I burst out. 'Your little boy's going to love this. Is it his birthday today?'

'Tomorrow.' He paused. 'He'll be twelve.' He frowned. 'You said *little* – you don't think this cake is too young for him, do you?'

I shook my head. 'Oh no. If it was me, I'd love it. If I was a boy, I mean . . . I mean, just because it's red, it doesn't mean it's a *girl's* cake or anything,' I added, to clarify things.

'A *girl's* cake?' The man was frowning at the cake now as if he was suddenly seeing it in a worrying new light.

'May, come and sit down!' Ben snapped at me, and that's when I noticed the man in the navy blue jacket and trousers who was making his way down our carriage, stopping at each passenger in turn.

I immediately jumped back into my seat beside my brother. '*Ben!*' I hissed. 'What are we going to do?'

Ben was taking out his wallet.

I stared at the ticket inspector as he got closer and

17

closer. He was smiling at the people who had tickets, acting all friendly.

Finally the ticket inspector was right beside us, checking the ticket of the man with the cake. Then it was our turn.

'Your tickets, sir?' He was looking at Ben.

'We had to run for the train so we didn't have time to get any,' Ben grunted. 'Can we buy them now, please?'

'You're meant to get to the station in time to buy them,' the man replied briskly. 'Where did you get on?'

Ben told him the name of our station and the man told him how much we owed. Just as I was thinking we'd got off lightly, Ben looked in his wallet and let out a gasp of alarm.

'What's wrong?' I asked, feeling my stomach lurch.

'I gave Lou most of my cash to get that shopping this morning,' Ben mumbled. 'I forgot.' His face was redder now as he faced the inspector. 'I'm sorry, but I don't think I've got enough on me.' He started to fumble in his wallet again as if he was hoping to find some extra money hidden somewhere in it – but of course he didn't. 'No . . . I'm five pounds short.' His voice was trembling slightly.

'Credit card?' the man asked. He wasn't looking friendly any more, I noticed.

Ben shook his head. We had started owing money on our bank cards recently, so Ben had made a point of putting them away in a drawer at home where he said they were staying until we'd paid them off.

The ticket inspector looked so grave that my tummy started to go crampy.

Suddenly the man across the aisle spoke. 'Here,' he said, holding out a ten-pound note. 'I'd like to contribute this to the cost of their fares.'

The ticket inspector looked at him in surprise. 'You sure you want to do that, sir?'

'Quite sure.'

I was so relieved I didn't know what to say, but I could tell Ben was feeling really humiliated. I dug my fingernails into his arm and whispered, 'It's OK, Ben.'

The inspector pushed a few buttons on his machine, handed us two return tickets to the seaside and gave my brother a five-pound note in change. Then, thankfully, he moved on up the train.

Ben immediately leaned over me to give the five pounds back to our neighbour.

But the man didn't put out his hand to take it. 'Do you have any money left if you give me that?' he asked.

'Not on me, but—'

'So what are you and your . . .' He looked at me, then back at Ben, enquiringly. '. . . sister, is it . . . ?'

Ben nodded.

'What are you and your sister going to do all day with no money?'

'We'll get on the next train and come straight back again,' Ben replied promptly.

'*No, Ben!*' I burst out before I could stop myself. I didn't want to go straight home again. Now that we were on the train, I wanted my day out. Besides, I was getting hungry and five pounds would at least buy us an ice cream and some chips each.

But Ben was still leaning across me, still holding

out the money. 'Look, we really appreciate you helping us, but we don't need this as well,' he said stiffly.

The man said quietly, 'Don't be silly. Your sister
has just saved me far more than ten pounds' worth
of cake and I would like to be allowed to reward her
for it.'

I looked at Ben, worried that he would object to
being called silly, but for once he didn't seem to mind
being spoken to as if he was less responsible than he
really was. He was eyeing the cake box and I knew
he was thinking that what the man was saying was
true. That cake would have cost far more to replace
than the money we were being offered. Slowly Ben
drew back his hand.

'Thank you,' I said, beaming at the man.

'That's quite all right.'

'Yeah . . . thanks,' Ben muttered. 'And I'm sorry
for . . . well . . . for . . .'

The man nodded as if he agreed that Ben *should*
be sorry. 'You could have got yourself into a lot of
bother,' he said, in a stern, slightly headmasterish
sort of way.

My brother flushed again and for an awful
moment I thought he might get really huffy and start
trying to give the money back all over again, but he
didn't. He just turned away quickly to look out the
window.

I wished I could tell this man – and everyone else
on the train – what a brilliant big brother Ben was
and how he'd always looked after me and how he
wasn't the sort of person who would normally get on
a train without paying. But I knew Ben would kill me
if I said anything at all, so I snuggled up close to him
instead, shutting my eyes and pretending we were so

rich that this was our own private train which nobody was allowed to ride on except us.

I guess I must have fallen asleep because the next thing I knew, we were pulling into our station. The man who had been sitting opposite us was gone, but he had left his newspaper behind. Even though it was just a local paper rather than one of the big national ones, Ben picked it up and tucked it under his arm to read later. Ben always picked up any reading material that people left lying around.

'Listen, May,' Ben said as we walked along the platform towards the station exit, 'that business with the tickets just now – it must have been horrible for you. I'm sorry. The thing is, I've not been thinking straight because of Lou.'

And, finally, Ben started to talk to me about my sister. He told me he couldn't bear the thought of going on living in our grotty flat without her any more than I could. 'If Lou's moving on, then I really want us to as well,' he said. 'Then it wouldn't feel as if we were being left behind. It'd feel like this was a new chapter in *all* our lives instead. You wouldn't have to go to that dump of a secondary school round the corner next year and I . . . well . . . maybe I could find something new and more interesting to do too.' Ben sighed, as if he felt like he hadn't done anything new or interesting in a very long time.

I nodded. 'But we haven't got enough money to go to India with Lou, have we?' I said.

'I don't mean that *we* should go off travelling too.' He paused. 'I just mean . . . I don't know . . . maybe I could get a proper job or something, so we could afford to live somewhere better.'

That's when something in the newspaper he was

21

carrying caught my eye. The page facing outwards was the local jobs section and one of the adverts was written in heavy bold print:

FULL-TIME EXPERIENCED GARDENER WANTED.
OWN COTTAGE WITH SALARY.

'Look, Ben!' I gasped, tugging the newspaper out from under his arm.

He read the advert slowly. 'I'm rubbish with plants,' he murmured, 'and I've never done any proper gardening in my life.'

'Still . . .' I said.

'*Still* . . .' he agreed.

And we looked at each other.

❋ 3 ❋

As soon as we got home from our day at the seaside, we started to hatch our plan. Ben was a bit uncertain after he'd had time to think about it some more, but Lou and I egged him on and pretty soon he'd agreed to at least phone up and make an initial enquiry about the gardening job.

We listened while he rang the number and spoke to the person at the other end. 'Yes . . . I have . . . er . . . several years' experience,' we heard him lie. 'Yes . . . I'm twenty-six . . . Single, yes . . . but I have a little sister who lives with me . . . Eleven . . . Yes, we would want to make use of the cottage . . . Right . . . Of course . . . Hang on, I'll fetch a pen . . .'

He looked despondent when he came off the phone. 'That was the housekeeper. I have to send a letter describing my previous experience and provide the name and address of at least one referee. I reckon I may as well forget it.'

Lou looked thoughtful. 'What about Miss Johnson?'

As well as working as a waitress, Lou had another job one day a week, helping an old blind lady called Miss Johnson. She went there every Wednesday when

Miss Johnson's live-in helper took her day off and sometimes I went with her if it was the school holidays. Occasionally Miss Johnson dictated letters for Lou to write sometimes, or else Lou read to her and chatted with her. Lou had got the job through Ben, who had been doing some painting work in Miss Johnson's house. Ben had done a good job and while he was there he had told Miss Johnson about Lou and me, and that's how Lou had ended up working there too.

'I didn't do any gardening for her,' Ben said.

'No, but they don't need to know that, do they? She'd give you a really good reference for the work you *did* do there. I could change what she says, just slightly. She always gets me to write her letters for her, remember. I could just add a line about you gardening. If I ask her for a reference for you on Wednesday, I bet she'll dictate it to me there and then. You could enclose it with your letter.'

'But it's . . .' Ben looked uncomfortable. '. . . it's really horrible, taking advantage of her like that . . .'

'It *is* pretty mean . . .' Lou mumbled, sounding less certain. And she looked at me as if she didn't like the fact that I was listening to this.

'Miss Johnson's been really good to us as well,' Ben added, frowning. He looked down at the job advert again. 'Our own cottage,' he said, and swallowed hard.

I could tell how torn Ben was feeling – and even though I wanted to go and live in that cottage too, I also wanted to make things easier for him. 'It's OK, Ben,' I said. 'We can just stay here, if you like. The school here isn't that bad.'

Ben just pulled a face like he thought it *was*. You

see, the secondary school I was due to start at after the summer – and the one Louise had switched to after we'd moved here – had a reputation for being pretty rough. I could stand up for myself at school and I had a gang of mates who were going there too, so I wasn't too worried about getting bullied. But Ben, who had been quite brainy at school and got three A levels, was worried I wouldn't get any at all, just like Louise, because apparently at that school hardly anybody did.

'It really is OK,' I attempted to reassure him. 'Even if I don't get any A levels, it doesn't matter since I don't want to go to university or anything.' I'd already told him I wasn't going to be swotty like him, even if my primary-school teachers *were* always banging on about how I had a lot of potential if only I'd work harder. It's being swotty that gets you picked on – at least it would with the mates *I* hung out with – and I intended to survive school, thanks very much. 'I mean, *you* didn't go to university, did you?' I added. 'And neither did Louise.'

That was the wrong thing to say. Ben's eyes were almost popping out of his head as he answered, 'I *could* have gone to university – that's the point! I got offered a place doing exactly what I wanted to do.' (The reason Ben hadn't taken up his place at university was that our mother had died just after he left school, so he'd ended up looking after me instead.) 'You might *want* to go to university when you're older, May,' he added fiercely, 'and if you get good enough exam results, *you'll* be able to.'

He turned to face Lou now, still looking furious. 'Did *anyone* in your year get any A levels, Lou?' he demanded. 'Well, did they?'

25

Lou was looking pretty upset herself. 'Look, Ben, if you feel so strongly about May's education, you'll have to do what I suggested. Otherwise, there's no point torturing yourself about it, is there, since you can't change anything?'

Or torturing me, I nearly added, but luckily I thought better of it.

Ben seemed to grit his teeth. 'OK, then,' he said. 'Let's do it!'

'You're sure?' Lou looked troubled.

'I want you to get me that reference.'

'May, can you leave us a minute, please?' Lou said firmly, keeping her eyes fixed on Ben.

I slipped away into my bedroom, feeling bad. I liked Miss Johnson and I could sense that, by deceiving her, our family was about to cross some sort of line that we'd all rather not cross. And Ben and Louise were doing this mainly for me, which made me feel like it was my fault, just like it had been my fault that Ben hadn't got to go to university. (When I'd said that to Ben once, he'd said I'd only been four at the time, so how could anything have been my fault? But sometimes, when he starts ranting on about how much he wants *me* to go to university one day, I can't help feeling that he *is* still angry about it and that he *is* taking it out on me in a funny sort of way.)

When I got home from school on Wednesday I paused in our hallway as I heard my brother and sister talking in the living room. Lou was telling Ben about the reference that Miss Johnson had dictated to her that afternoon and they didn't seem to have heard me come in. I had a feeling they might not want me listening in to their conversation, so I stayed in the hall and kept quiet. Lou was telling Ben that she'd only had to tweak the wording on his reference a little bit, as well as substituting the word *gardener* for *painter and decorator*, and that she'd made out that Miss Johnson had known Ben for five years instead of just two, because she said that would mean Ben wouldn't be expected to provide earlier references as well.

'See what you think,' she told him, and she began to read it out loud. 'TO WHOM THIS MAY CONCERN . . . I would highly recommend Benjamin Duthie as a gardener. I have known him for five years and he is extremely conscientious, reliable and courteous, and his work over this time has proved to be of a very high standard. Being blind, I am unable to comment first hand on the appearance of his work, but many trusted friends assure me of its high quality and of his obvious attention to detail. As regards his character, I think it worth adding that Benjamin is an honest, responsible young man who has cared for his younger sister since the death of their mother. I can also vouch for the good character of both his sisters, the older of whom is also in my employ.' She paused.

'Miss Johnson must really like you, to say all that, Ben,' I called out, as I dumped my school bag down noisily to let them know I was back.

'When did *you* get home?' Lou asked as I joined them.

'Just now. Didn't you hear me come in? Really, Ben, she must like you a *lot*,' I repeated, as I went over to look more closely at the letter Lou was holding.

Although it was written in my sister's handwriting, Miss Johnson had signed it at the bottom and it was written on her special headed notepaper, which gave her address. Her house had a posh name, which made it sound even grander than it really was, and it was situated in a village a few miles away from where we lived, where all the houses were expensive ones with big gardens.

'*Louise* must like me a lot, you mean,' Ben said drily.

'No, Ben, I told you, I hardly changed any of it,' Lou protested. 'She was the one who said all that stuff about your good character and everything.'

'I feel really mean, conning her like this.' Ben was frowning. 'Especially after she's gone on about how trustworthy I am.'

'What would happen to you if anyone found out?' I asked my brother suddenly. For the first time I was worried that Ben might get into really serious trouble if he got caught faking his reference.

But Louise didn't give Ben a chance to answer me. 'Look, Ben, do you want to get May out of this grotty flat and into a better school or not?'

'You know I do.'

'Well, you're doing this for a good reason then, aren't you? Look, if Miss Johnson knew why you wanted to move, she might even dictate you a false reference herself,' Lou said, as she slipped the reference into the envelope along with the covering letter Ben had written.

Ben's letter was typed out – he'd used the computer in our local library to do it – and it was very neat. Ben's good at writing because English was one of the A-level subjects he did at the grammar school

28

he went to. He did history too, which is the subject he liked best of all and the one he'd been planning to study at university. We'd lived in a better area then, but apparently our mother had had lots of debts, which was why we'd had to move here after she died. Lou says our mother wasn't very good at managing money, and that that's the reason Ben is so careful with it himself.

'Now all you have to do is find out everything you can about gardening,' Lou added, when our brother remained silent.

'I suppose I *could* go next door and speak to Arthur,' Ben grunted. Arthur was our next-door neighbour and he had an allotment nearby, where he grew vegetables.

'Good idea! We'll go and post your letter to Thornton Hall while you're doing that,' Lou offered. (Thornton Hall was the name of the house that had advertised for a gardener.) 'Then we'll go to the library and get you some gardening books.'

As my sister and I arrived at the postbox outside our flats, ten minutes later, I said, 'Remember when Ben killed that plant by giving it aspirin?' Ben had once given one of Lou's favourite houseplants a drink of soluble aspirin because he thought he'd read in some newspaper article that aspirin was good for plants, when really it was some kind of *cut* flowers the article had been talking about. Lou's plant had died a spectacularly squidgy death and Lou had been really angry and made all sorts of threats about what she'd do to Ben if he ever touched a green living thing that belonged to her ever again.

Louise laughed. (The aspirin incident had become

a family joke now.) 'It's true that Ben's never exactly been green-fingered, has he?' she replied.

'So do you think it's *safe* to let him be a gardener?' I asked her.

She laughed again. 'Maybe not right now, but I wouldn't worry. He's a real swot when it comes to studying, so I'm sure a few gardening books will turn him into an expert in no time!'

A big pink graffiti heart had been sprayed on to the side of the postbox by one of my friends, and I pointed it out to Lou proudly as we dropped Ben's letter inside.

'Very nice,' she said, not sounding as if she thought it was nice at all. 'God, I can't wait to get out of this dump.'

'I'm sure if Ben *does* get this job, there'll be room for you to come and live with us in the cottage too,' I said hopefully. 'If you change your mind about going travelling, I mean.'

'I'm not changing my mind, May,' Lou replied, frowning.

We didn't talk much on the bus, and when we got to the library we headed straight for the gardening section and chose three books we thought might help Ben.

'Let's get a film out as well, shall we?' Lou suggested then. 'We can watch it tonight.' She knew how much I loved it when she stayed in to watch TV with me instead of going out with Greg on her nights off, so I guessed she was making a special effort to cheer me up.

We went across to look at the DVDs and Lou immediately chose an old black-and-white film called *Rebecca*, which she said I was really going to like because it was all about a girl who went to live in a massive old house where there were lots of secrets. Apparently it was based on a book that Lou had read and thought was brilliant.

'It sounds a bit like *The Secret Garden*,' I said, and she nodded. But then I saw from the picture on the box that the main character wasn't a girl my age at all, but a young woman, Lou's age, and I knew Lou was just trying to get me to agree to watch what *she* wanted as usual. I tried to put it back and take out *Bride of Dracula* instead, but she wouldn't let me.

'You're too young for that. It'll give you nightmares,' she said firmly. She was looking across at the computer section. Since we didn't have a computer at home, we tended to use the ones in the library quite a lot. 'I know . . . let's set you up with your own email address while we're here. Then we can email each other while I'm away. You can tell me all about what you're doing and we can have proper girly chats, no matter what country I'm in! It'll be fun!'

'Not as much fun as if you stayed here with us,' I *nearly* replied. But I stopped myself. She'd explained to me why she had to go and I knew she really wanted me to understand that. So I felt like I had no choice but to try.

After we'd cleared away the dishes that evening, Lou persuaded Ben to stop studying his gardening books so that we could all watch *Rebecca* together. I thought it would be boring, and I'd made up my mind only to watch it for as long as it took to eat the chocolate Lou had bought for the film. But in the end, I sort of got into it. It's all about this young woman who marries a rich older man and goes to live with him in this

31

huge old house by the sea where he used to live with his first wife – Rebecca – who died tragically, only to start with you don't know exactly how. And there's this really sinister housekeeper, all dressed in black, called Mrs Danvers, who never smiles and who taunts the girl by telling her how perfect and beautiful Rebecca was.

'I hope the housekeeper at Thornton Hall isn't like her,' Ben joked when we got to the part in the film where the girl is really upset and Mrs Danvers tells her she'd be better off dead and tries to persuade her to jump out of an upstairs window. 'She sounded pretty scary on the phone.'

'What's her name?' I asked.

'Mrs Daniels,' he replied.

Lou and I both looked up.

'You're kidding,' Lou said.

He shook his head.

'Daniels, not *Danvers*,' I pointed out.

'Still . . .' Lou grinned. Then she started to giggle. Lou's giggles are infectious and soon Ben and I were joining in.

'I won't be able to keep a straight face if I have to meet this Danvers woman now,' Ben gasped, when he finally stopped laughing.

'You mean, *Daniels* woman,' I corrected him.

Lou let out a snort, and then we were laughing again, so loudly that you'd never think we were about to set off into the unknown, where things would never be the same old, just-the-three-of-us way they were now, ever again.

✳ 4 ✳

On the morning Lou was due to leave, I switched on my videotape of *The Secret Garden* and listened to the bit with the oboe music while Lou was putting the last few things into her backpack. At the start of *The Secret Garden*, Mary's mother and father have just died, but she doesn't feel bad about it because she hardly knew them. And I might as well mention now that that's how I feel about my parents too.

I was four when my mother died and I can hardly remember her at all. Ben and Louise have told me things about her, of course. Apparently she used to stay in bed a lot after Ben and Louise's dad left her, and when she eventually started going out again she dated a few different men – one of whom must have been my father. I came along after a while, as a 'lovely, unexpected surprise', according to Louise. My mother never told Lou and Ben who my father was so, like I said before, I've always counted *him* as sort of non-existent.

After my mother got ill with cancer when I was still a baby, I went to live with foster carers on and off. I can't remember any of that. As soon as he was old enough, Ben took care of me instead, and when our mother died he was allowed to keep me. He says that's because the people who decide these things realized he was the person I was most attached to. Of course, I was also attached to Louise, who was fifteen by then. She stayed with us too, because she didn't want to go and live with her dad and his girlfriend who she didn't like very much. We had a social worker for a while – I remember her coming to visit us sometimes – but then, as we all got older, social services left us alone.

So you see, even though I didn't have any parents, I'd always had my brother and sister and I'd always felt loved and looked after and *wanted*. Until now . . .

Of course, I knew *why* Lou was leaving. She'd explained it to me as best she could. I knew it wasn't because she didn't love me, and I also knew that it wasn't as if she was going away for good, because she'd be back by this time next year. But somehow it still felt as if she *was* going away forever, because when she came back she wouldn't be living with me and Ben any more. She had already told me that too.

Ben and I went to the train station to see her and Greg off. First they had to catch the train to London, then they were flying to India from Heathrow. They both had enormous backpacks and Lou was complaining about how heavy hers was. Greg, who had been backpacking before, felt the weight of it himself and said, 'My God, what have you got in here?' which made Lou burst into tears.

She wasn't crying because of her backpack though. She was crying because she was saying goodbye.

'You don't need to stay away for a whole year if you don't like it when you get there,' I told her, as I tried to stop blubbing myself.

She smiled at me through her tears, but she didn't say anything back.

Ben looked upset too, but he didn't cry – he never does.

Greg looked embarrassed as he busied himself with loading their backpacks on to the train while we finished our farewells. His parents lived in London so they were going to meet him at the airport to say goodbye.

When the London train had disappeared from view and I had nothing to wave at any more Ben put his arm round me. 'A year isn't that long, you know,' he mumbled, sounding like he was trying to convince himself as much as me. 'Think how quickly *this* year's passed.'

But I didn't think the past year had gone by that quickly at all.

As we were leaving the station Ben's mobile phone started ringing. I immediately thought it was Lou, calling us from the train to say goodbye again, but it wasn't. It was the housekeeper from Thornton Hall. Ben had given both his numbers when he'd sent in his job application.

'Hello . . . Yes . . . Mrs Daniels . . . ? No, it's OK . . . What . . . ? OK . . . Thank you . . . Sure . . . We'll be there!'

He came off the phone, looking like he didn't know whether to smile or freak out. 'They want me to go for an interview at Thornton Hall the day after tomorrow,' he said. 'And since you'll be living in the cottage as well if I get the job, they want to meet you too.'

*

35

It turned out that Thornton Hall was situated in a village called Lower Thornton, which was very near the seaside town we'd visited two weeks earlier. In fact, it was only one stop before it on the train, so we ended up doing almost the same journey to get there. Thankfully, when we had our tickets checked this time it was by a different inspector. Ben said he didn't care if we met the same one again – but I could tell he would have been embarrassed really.

'Ben, what happened when you got caught fare-dodging that time when you were fourteen?' I suddenly wanted to know.

Ben pulled a face as if he didn't like remembering that time very much. 'I had to pay a fine, and Mum and Dad got told, of course. Mum wasn't too bothered, but Dad went ballistic. He whacked me pretty hard and said if I did it again he'd force me to live with him instead of with Mum, so he could make sure I got the discipline I needed. That was in the days when we actually saw him once a week, before he moved up north with his new girlfriend.' He grimaced. 'Funny thing is, even though he'd just laid into me, I missed him back then, so that actually felt like quite a tempting offer.'

'Really?' I was amazed, because this was the first time Ben had ever mentioned actually missing his dad. 'Did you *tell* him you wanted to live with him?'

He shook his head. 'I was too scared what Mum would do if I left her. She'd never managed all that well since Dad left – and then she got pregnant with you and the bloke didn't want to . . . well . . .' My brother paused for several moments.

'Didn't want to know,' I prompted him, because I'd grown up with Lou telling me this story and it didn't shock me. I'd certainly never thought of 'the bloke' Ben was referring to as my father, because Louise had told me ages ago that I didn't have to. She'd said that sometimes people helped to make babies without actually wanting to go on to be fathers or mothers to them and that was just the way things were. And since 'the bloke' who had helped to make *me* fell into that category, Louise's opinion was that he didn't count as any sort of father at all. Ben hadn't liked it when he'd heard Louise saying that to me, I remembered now. He'd accused her of over-simplifying things. But I liked the way Louise made everything in my life seem so matter-of-fact and uncomplicated.

'Yeah, well . . . after that, Mum *really* needed looking after,' Ben continued. 'I knew I couldn't let Dad haul me off with him then. I knew I couldn't get into any more trouble with the police either. My criminal career was kind of off the cards after that, see, because I knew Mum wouldn't cope if I got thrown into jail.' He gave an awkward little laugh.

'I don't think *I* could cope if you got thrown into jail either,' I pointed out, momentarily wondering if you could get sent to prison for saying you were a gardener when you weren't. He didn't answer me, and when I looked at him he was clearly lost in his own private thoughts.

Ben had been sent directions that involved walking a short way up the road from Lower Thornton station, then turning left and walking up the hill until we came to an open driveway with big stone gateposts on either side.

'This place should be called *Upper* Thornton,' I complained, stopping after our long trudge uphill to stare at the black plaque on the wall that said 'Thornton Hall' in gold lettering.

Ben didn't reply. He was so nervous now we were actually here that he had stopped speaking to me completely. The white gravel driveway leading up to the house was edged on both sides by neatly cut grass. To the left beyond the grass was a low wooden fence, on the other side of which was an empty field. To our right the grass gave way to an area of large leafy bushes and Ben started muttering that they were probably rhododendrons, only he couldn't be sure since they weren't flowering, and that he wished he'd brought his gardening books with him. The driveway was cut in a bend and as we followed it, keeping to the edge and taking care not to step on the grass, we suddenly saw the house straight ahead of us.

Ben swore under his breath. I went weak at the knees too. The house was enormous. It was built of light grey stone and the main part was oblong-shaped with two storeys and a low sloping roof. Another wing had been added to the left half of the building, so that it jutted out at the front. There was a sort of square tower at the left end of the main part of the house – perched quite awkwardly at the point where the two bits of the house met. The front porch, which wasn't central, but set to the right of the building, had four large stone pillars with some kind of climbing plant twisting around them. I started to count the windows. There were eight downstairs and ten upstairs – and those were only the ones at the front.

I glanced sideways at Ben and saw that he wasn't looking at the house any more. He was staring around us at the grounds. There was a lot of grass, which had to be a good thing surely, because even Ben knew how to work a lawnmower. But there were also some rose beds closer to the house and there were several stone troughs full of flowers beneath the ground-floor windows.

'Better not put any aspirin in those,' I joked.

Normally when anyone mentions that, Ben always starts laughing, but today he just looked at me as if he was going to be sick.

'Don't worry, Ben! I'm sure you'll get this job!' I burst out. He *had* to get it, because now that I had seen Thornton Hall I didn't want to leave. Leaving now would be like Mary in *The Secret Garden* getting shipped back to India before the story had even begun.

'The main gardens must be round the back,' Ben was saying in a shaky voice. 'I bet they're huge! God, how I am ever going to get through this?'

I knew I had to stop him panicking or he was going to muck up his interview. 'Look, what's the worst thing that can happen?' I asked him, because that's what Lou always says whenever either of us is getting stressed out about anything.

Ben gave me a funny look as if he didn't like me speaking to him like Lou would. 'The worst thing is that they'll think I'm not a very good gardener and they'll employ somebody else,' he answered. 'And if I'm lucky they won't report me to the police for faking my reference.' He held up the letter he'd been sent confirming the details of the interview. 'It says we've to go to the front door,' he said. 'You'd think as servants we'd have to go round the back, wouldn't you?'

We went up to the porch and Ben rang the bell. We couldn't hear it ringing inside the house and I wanted him to ring it again, but he wouldn't. He thought it might have rung where we couldn't hear it, so that his pressing it again would sound impatient. Eventually, after we'd been standing there for ages, even he had to admit that he probably hadn't pressed it hard enough the first time, so he tried again, and this time we heard it ring inside the hall quite clearly.

Almost immediately the door was opened and we found ourselves standing face to face with . . . and I'm really not making this up . . . *the* terrifying housekeeper from *Rebecca*. Or at least a very close replica of her. She looked a little older and greyer than the housekeeper who had been so scary in the film, but otherwise she could have been her twin. She had thick dark grey hair pulled back in a bun, thick dark eyebrows and the same fierce dark eyes that seemed to pierce right through into your brain. She was even wearing a totally black dress.

I let out a gasp of shock. Then – to my dismay – I felt bubbles of laughter start to rise in my throat. I could feel Ben next to me, making the connection too. I knew he was struggling to keep his voice steady as he said, 'I'm Benjamin Duthie – here about the gardening job.'

The housekeeper said in a crisp voice, 'I am Mrs Daniels.'

I let it out first – I couldn't stop myself. It came out as an explosive laugh right in her face. I quickly turned away, covering my mouth with my hands. I stumbled off the porch and headed off down the drive, hoping that if I removed myself from the scene,

Ben would somehow manage to keep himself under control. But to my horror, behind me, I could hear my brother letting out a snort of laughter too.

I kept walking blindly away from the house. This was all my fault. If I hadn't laughed first, then I wouldn't have set Ben off. I had seen the look the housekeeper had given me. Now she would be giving that same look to my brother. Soon she would be informing her employer that Ben had laughed in her face and was clearly an unsuitable candidate for the job.

I was halfway down the drive, knowing that I had to stop and wait for Ben but feeling completely unable to face him, when a car horn sounded in front of me. I looked up to see a large black vehicle slowing to a halt directly ahead of me. A stern middle-aged man was sitting at the wheel – a stern middle-aged man I recognized. He leaned out of the car window, clearly recognizing me too, as he exclaimed in a surprised voice, 'It's Mary, isn't it? What are *you* doing here?'

It was the man from the train – the one whose cake I had saved.

As he got out of his car I noticed that he wasn't alone. A boy about my own age, with a plump freckly face and curly hair, was sitting in the front passenger seat. I didn't do more than glance at him though. I was too busy staring at the man.

'Mary, what are you doing here?' he repeated.

'I've just ruined everything!' I blurted out. 'I made Ben laugh and now he won't get the gardening job and we won't be able to come and live here!' And maybe because he was someone familiar, in a totally unfamiliar place, I burst into tears.

'Mary . . .' He put a hand on my shoulder, then

41

seemed to feel awkward doing that and quickly removed it again. He turned to speak to the boy in the car. 'Alex, why don't you go on up to the house? Tell Mrs Daniels I won't be long.'

I heard the sound of heavy feet scrunching on gravel as the boy did as he was told. The man leaned back against the bonnet of his car and said, 'Now, tell me . . . I can hardly believe this . . . but is it *your* brother who's applied for the job as gardener here?'

I nodded.

'Well, I never!' He was shaking his head in disbelief.

'But what are *you* doing here?' I asked, sniffing.

'Thornton Hall is my house.'

'But it can't be! *You're* the man from the train!' I knew it was a dumb thing to say, but he didn't respond as if it was. He seemed to understand.

'It *is* a remarkable coincidence that we should meet again like this,' he agreed, frowning. 'I don't think I introduced myself properly when we met before, did I? My name is Michael Rutherford – and I assume that the Benjamin Duthie who's applied for the job here is the young man I met with you the other day?'

I nodded. Suddenly I remembered that the job advert had been in the newspaper that the man with the cake – Mr Rutherford – had been reading. It had even been open at the right page, which was how I had spotted it. Now I knew why. Mr Rutherford must have been checking his *own* advert – the one *he* had put in to try and find a gardener. So, in a way, our meeting up again like this wasn't a coincidence at all. It was *because* we had met him that day – and picked up his newspaper – that we were here.

But before I could explain that he continued, 'But, Mary, why are you so upset?'

'Because . . . because . . . we went to the door and . . . and . . .'

'What?' he prompted me, when I gave up speaking completely. 'Surely my housekeeper isn't *that* fearsome?'

That was too much for me. I told him everything – how we'd got out the film of *Rebecca* from the library and how we'd joked that we hoped Mrs *Daniels* wasn't anything like Mrs *Danvers* because Mrs *Danvers* was really scary. I started to explain a bit about the story then, in case he'd never seen the film, but he interrupted me to say that he had watched the film *and* read the book and so he was quite familiar with the plot of *Rebecca*.

I sniffed. 'So . . . so when Mrs Danvers opened the door to us here . . . I mean Mrs *Daniels* opened the door to us . . . and she was all dressed in black and all fierce-looking like in the film . . . well . . . we . . . we . . . *I* . . . started to laugh . . . And Ben couldn't help laughing because when someone else laughs it's very infectious, Lou says. Anyway, now Mrs Daniels won't want you to give Ben the job, will she?'

Mr Rutherford was leaning back against his car bonnet looking like he was struggling not to smile himself. 'Mrs Danvers and Mrs Daniels seem to have *both* made quite an impression on you,' he said. 'Though I must admit that Mrs Daniels does look rather severe in that black dress she's wearing today. Come to think of it, she always looks severe when I'm interviewing new gardeners. I think it might be because—'

'Mrs Daniels isn't in *mourning*, is she?' I burst out before he could finish.

'I beg your pardon?'

'Mrs Danvers wore black because she was in mourning for Rebecca. So I just thought maybe Mrs *Daniels* was in mourning for somebody too.'

'Well . . .' He looked a bit surprised by my question. 'My aunt owned this house before she died last year, and Mrs Daniels was her housekeeper for a long time. I moved here only a few months ago, you see. But I'm fairly sure my aunt's death isn't the reason—'

'Because if it *is* the reason,' I interrupted him again, 'Mrs Daniels could try wearing your aunt's favourite colour instead. You can do that at funerals – wear the person's favourite colour instead of black, to show them that you're thinking about them. That's what my big sister did at our mother's funeral. She wore a bright red dress. She says a lot of people stared at her but she didn't care because she was doing it for our mum.'

Mr Rutherford looked like our conversation was making his head spin a bit. 'I see . . . well . . . that makes sense . . . except that I don't think suggesting that Mrs Daniels wears my aunt's favourite colour would be a very good idea.'

'Why? Would she get angry?' I suddenly wondered if Mr Rutherford was more afraid of his housekeeper than he was letting on.

'No,' he replied, 'but I'm almost certain that my aunt's favourite colour *was* black. That's the colour she always wore when *I* came to see her, in any case! Whereas I think you'll find that Mrs Daniels does occasionally wear navy blue.'

He definitely had an amused twinkle in his eye as he got back into his car. 'I really must go and interview my prospective gardeners now, Mary, but don't worry. I shall bear in mind what you've just told me if Mrs Daniels has any complaints about your brother. You can go round to the back of the house to wait for him, if you like. There's a swing there you might like to play on. I got it for my son but he doesn't ever seem to use it.'

As he drove the short distance up the driveway I remembered the boy who had been in the car with him – presumably the same boy whose birthday cake I had rescued. If Ben got the job here, I might meet him again, I thought.

I headed across the grass, making for the back of the house as Mr Rutherford had suggested. Maybe now, since I had explained *why* we had laughed at Mrs Daniels, Ben was still in with a chance.

Then I realized something else. Mr Rutherford had first met Ben that day on the train when Ben had been caught without enough money to pay for our tickets. First impressions were very important – Ben was always saying that. And since Mr Rutherford's first impression of Ben must have been that he was either totally scatterbrained or totally dishonest, how could he possibly want to give Ben this job?

✳ 5 ✳

I stopped where I was as I faced up to the truth. Ben wasn't going to get a job here and we were never going to get to move here. It didn't even matter that we'd laughed when Mrs Daniels opened the front door. It didn't matter because Mr Rutherford wasn't going to employ Ben in any case. There was no point in my brother even going ahead with his interview.

I knew I had to find Ben and warn him – but how? I could always ring the front doorbell and just ask to speak to him – but I didn't think I could face Mrs Daniels again.

I headed round the side of the house, crouching down low as I peered in through each window, trying to spot my brother. There were five windows in total on this side of the building. The first three all looked into one enormous sitting room, which had three windows facing the front as well. The room was filled with old-fashioned furniture, flowery rugs and fussy ornaments that I guessed must have belonged to Mr Rutherford's aunt.

The fourth window looked into a different room. I immediately felt my heart beating faster because there, standing in front of a bookcase examining the books, was Ben. He wasn't alone though. Seated at a long table in the middle of the room was another, much older man. I assumed he must be one of the other applicants for the job.

Just as I was about to knock on the window to get Ben's attention, Mrs Daniels walked in and I quickly crouched down lower. When I stood up again, Ben was following her out. She must be taking him for his interview with Mr Rutherford and it was too late for me to do anything to stop it.

It took nearly forty-five minutes for the interview to be over, and during that time I sat on the swing, biting my fingernails.

When Ben finally emerged from the house, I thought he'd be looking upset or embarrassed, but he wasn't.

The first thing he said was, 'The man from the train!'

'I know! I met him in the drive. What did he say to you?'

'Well, first he asked me how I'd heard about the job, so I told him I'd picked up the newspaper he'd left behind. He seemed to find that quite amusing.'

'Did he tell you off again, for getting on the train without paying?'

Ben looked irritated. 'No, May, he didn't *tell me off*!' He paused. 'Actually it was pretty awful at first. I felt like walking straight out the second I saw who he was. But it was like he was expecting me to want to do that, and he wasn't having any of it. He told me really firmly to sit down – and I did – and then he told me he'd met you outside. He wanted to know all about us – how I came to be looking after you – all that sort of stuff. He asked me how I'd got myself into that situation on the train that day, so I told him the truth. We talked a bit about Lou leaving. Oh, and he asked me how I'd done at school as well. I wasn't expecting him to be interested in that. It turns out he used to teach history himself. He's written a couple of history books and he used to be a lecturer at a university, but he took early retirement when his aunt died last year and left him Thornton Hall in her will. Now he's going to live here and write more books. He seemed pretty impressed when I told him my A-level results – especially the history one! He said he was surprised I hadn't gone on to further education, so I told him I hadn't really had the opportunity at the time. He asked how I'd got into gardening and I told him gardening had just sort of found *me* rather than the other way round. Now *that* wasn't lying, was it?'

'Did he ask you any questions you couldn't answer?' I asked, holding my breath.

'Gardening questions, you mean? No, that was the weird thing. He sort of got all caught up in talking about history. I don't think he knows much about gardening himself, in any case, because all he asked was if I thought I could manage the gardens here, and when I said yes, he went back to asking me what aspects of history I was especially interested in.'

'So do you think he'll give you the job?' I asked. I couldn't understand how Ben could still be in the running after everything that had happened, but it sounded like – by some miracle – he was.

'I don't know. He's got to interview the other guy first. Apparently the third person dropped out. But since we're the only ones who'd want to make use of the cottage, he's asked Mrs Daniels to show it to us now, in case we don't like it and want to withdraw our application or something.'

'Why? Is it a really horrible cottage?' I hadn't thought of that possibility.

'No one's lived in it for over a year apparently. Oh, and get this – apparently Mrs Daniels' husband used to be the gardener here before—'

He broke off as Mrs Daniels suddenly appeared in front of us, holding a big bunch of keys.

'My late husband was the gardener here for fifteen years,' Mrs Daniels informed us coolly, having obviously overheard Ben. 'We lived in the cottage until he passed away eight years ago.' She paused. 'No other gardener has lasted very long here since then.' She started to walk away from us, her fingers curled tightly around the keys.

'*Why* has no other gardener lasted very long here?' I whispered urgently to Ben, but he had already scurried after her.

'You live in the main house now, don't you, Mrs Daniels?' Ben was saying in his most carefully polite voice, clearly trying his hardest to make up for laughing at her earlier. 'Mr Rutherford says you know the house even better than he does.'

'I know the grounds better too,' she replied sharply. 'I know exactly how these gardens are meant to look. I soon knew when those other gardeners weren't doing their job properly.'

Ben swallowed. 'The gardens look OK to me,' he mumbled.

'The lawns have been cut recently, that's all. My Geoffrey would turn in his grave if he could see the state his gardens are in now.' She led us on down the front driveway, but before we got to the bottom she turned off along a narrow footpath. 'You can also reach the cottage from the main road,' she told us, 'but this way is quicker if you're coming from the house.'

The path cut through an overgrown bushy area before eventually emerging into an open space where we found ourselves staring straight ahead at the gardener's cottage. It was made of the same light grey stone as the house itself and had little latticed windows. From the outside it was just as I'd imagined it – apart from not having any roses growing round the door.

'Wait here,' Mrs Daniels told us as she turned the key in the lock.

But I couldn't wait. Less than a minute after she'd gone into the cottage, I followed her. I stepped excitedly into the little hallway and, to my surprise, found Mrs Daniels on her hands and knees on the living-room floor, peering under the settee as if she was searching for something. Her skirt had risen up and I could see the tops of her stockings and her suspenders.

'What are you doing?' I asked curiously. Ben, who had followed me inside, was tugging at my arm to pull me away, but I ignored him.

Mrs Daniels stumbled to her feet, looking cross. 'I thought I told you to wait outside,' she snapped, 'but clearly there's no point asking you to do anything you don't want to, is there, madam?'

Ben cleared his throat awkwardly. 'Sorry . . . Er . . . Perhaps if we just take a quick look round? Then we can get out of your way.'

'Go ahead. You clearly don't need *my* permission

to come in.' She brushed past us, heading back out through the front door.

We quickly looked over the rest of the cottage. It was clean enough, though the carpets and wallpaper were old-fashioned, with too many swirly patterns on them for my liking. The kitchen had a cooker, a sink, a washing machine, some old-fashioned Formica-topped units and an ancient-looking fridge that was unplugged and standing with its door wedged open. The bathroom had a bath, sink and toilet, but no shower. There were two small bedrooms, both with dark wooden wardrobes and chests of drawers, with a double bed in one and a single bed in the other. The room with the single bed had a window that looked out on to the garden of the cottage and through the trees you could just make out the tower of the main house. I tried hard to imagine the bedroom with my curtains and duvet and bright fluffy cushions from home. Maybe it would look OK.

We went back into the living room and had another look in there, at the heavy maroon sofa and matching armchair, the square dining table with its four non-matching chairs and the big ugly sideboard. It all looked like it had come from one of those second-hand shops where they sell off the furniture of old people who've died.

'I can always redecorate,' Ben said, as if he could tell what I was thinking. 'Tell you what . . . if we get the place, I'll paint your room first, OK?'

I nodded, feeling more hopeful. 'OK! And at least we've got throws to cover the sofa.' Lou had always been big on using brightly coloured throws to cover the tatty bits of furniture we had in our flat.

'Well?' Mrs Daniels asked as we stepped outside

into the sunshine again. She was looking hopeful too – hopeful that we might have been put off wanting to live here. I guessed that meant that she still hadn't forgiven us for laughing at her earlier. (Like I already said, Ben is always going on about how first impressions make a big impact on people and I reckoned Mrs Daniels was proving him right, even if Mr Rutherford wasn't.)

'It's fine, thanks,' Ben replied politely. 'I'm going to take May down to the village now for some lunch. Mr Rutherford said he'd let me know about the job later this afternoon so we'll come back then, if that's OK.'

Mrs Daniels nodded. 'The food in the tea room isn't up to much,' she said. 'You'll do better in the pub. They'll let your sister in, so long as you sit in the garden.'

'Right,' Ben said. 'Thanks.'

As we turned to go she suddenly added, 'I was checking for mice under the sofa just now. There were some droppings when I came in to look the place over the other day.'

'Yuck!' I pulled a face.

Mrs Daniels' face was grim. 'I didn't think you'd like it. That's why I asked you to wait outside. It doesn't matter though. We can get the pest-control people in if necessary. Unless you've got a cat?'

Ben shook his head.

'Shame.'

As we walked off down the driveway to the road, Ben whispered, 'I reckon Mrs Daniels could scare mice away better than any cat.'

And I giggled my agreement.

*

There was one tea shop in the village, situated just across from the train station in a little row of shops that also contained a newsagent's, a hardware shop, a chemist's and a small foodstore. We had spotted the pub on our way down the road, but somehow we both felt it was safer to do the opposite of what Mrs Daniels had recommended.

'The pub is probably well known for giving you food poisoning or something,' Ben said. 'That's probably why she wants us to eat there – so we don't actually make it back this afternoon.'

As we went inside the tea room, a bell rang above the door. It was past lunchtime and the place was empty apart from one couple who were in the process of leaving. We sat down at the window table and waited to be served. The tables all had white lacy cloths with white plastic ones underneath. The white lacy one on our table had stains on it and looked like it could do with a wash.

Normally when we eat out Ben doesn't chat much to the staff, apart from maybe asking something about the food. But today the lady who took our order asked us all about ourselves before she even asked what we wanted to eat, so he ended up telling her that we had just come from Thornton Hall and that he was applying for a job as gardener there.

That brought the other lady in the tea room over to our table. The two of them introduced themselves as Kathy and Barbara, and it turned out that they were sisters who lived in the village and ran the shop together. They hadn't really known Mr Rutherford's aunt who had died last year, but they did know Mrs Daniels.

'Snooty piece of work, she is!' the lady called Kathy

said. 'The last time she came in here, she complained about my scones! I'd think twice before you take any gardening job there, if I were you. Jimmy, our cousin's lad, was the last gardener they employed. He's only just left the place. Apparently that Daniels woman was always making out he didn't cut the mustard compared with her late husband—'

'– whose name you'll never hear the last of if you take that job,' her sister added.

'Exactly so – and in the end poor Jimmy got sick of hearing how her Geoffrey did this and how her Geoffrey did that, so he handed in his notice.'

'Really?' Ben was looking thoughtful, as if he reckoned that having Mrs Daniels telling him exactly how her husband used to do things in the garden would be a blessing in disguise if *he* got the job.

'Did Jimmy live in the gardener's cottage?' I asked them.

'Goodness, no! He lived with his mother in the village. You don't want anything to do with that cottage, let me tell you!'

'Now, Kathy . . .' her sister began, but the woman was clearly on a roll and there was no stopping her.

'They might as well know what they're dealing with, Barbara!' She pulled out a seat from the table next to us and sat down. 'Mrs Daniels moved out of that cottage and into the big house with the old lady just after her husband died. Thick as thieves, those two were after that! Mrs Daniels was given a whole suite of rooms there, all to herself, so people say. Well, over the years a few other gardeners came and went – some stayed in that cottage and some didn't, but nobody made it their home for very long. *She* was always hostile towards them, so I've heard. Then, nearly a year ago, the old lady dies, leaving Mrs Daniels up there on her own, acting like she owns the place. That's until the old lady's nephew moves in a few months ago. Well, it's around that time that the weird goings-on start . . .' She paused dramatically.

I was getting excited now. I felt like I'd landed right in the middle of a proper adventure – as if I really was Mary Lennox in *The Secret Garden*.

'*What* weird goings-on?' I asked breathlessly.

'Lights in the cottage when it's meant to be empty. And noises!' Kathy had lowered her voice to a whisper.

'Maybe someone's been squatting there,' Ben suggested.

'That's what Jimmy thought – he told that Rutherford chap straight away and they checked it out together, but they didn't find anything. Then Jimmy was walking past one night and he saw the lights again. Mr Rutherford was away that week so Jimmy went to investigate and he swears that he heard voices coming from inside the cottage. He knocked on the door and who should open it but Mrs Daniels herself. She got all cross with him and told him she'd just popped in to check up on the place. She said it was just her in there – nobody else – though Jimmy reckoned otherwise.' Kathy paused for breath, but not for long. 'Then, about a week later, she comes in here for a cream tea – which she has the nerve to complain about, would you believe? – and I ask her about that cottage myself. I tell her our Jimmy's a sensitive boy, but he's not the type to imagine things. And she actually *says* to me that she knows that, and that *she* wouldn't be surprised if it isn't her late husband's ghost causing all the racket everyone's been hearing in the cottage. She says she reckons her Geoffrey might not be able to rest in peace on account of the mess all those other gardeners – including our Jimmy – have been making of his life's work since he passed on.'

'Ach – she was having you on!' her sister said.

'You should've seen the look she gave me. If that's her having a joke, I wouldn't like to get too near to her when she's being serious!'

I could see that Ben wasn't too impressed by their story, and I didn't believe in ghosts either, but I was still very curious to know what had *really* been happening in the cottage.

After Kathy had gone off into the kitchen and Barbara had brought us our lunch and was starting to clear the other tables, Ben asked, 'Excuse me, but I was wondering . . . do you know what the local secondary school is like?'

'Oh, it's very good,' Barbara replied, turning to face us again. 'My son went there.' She explained how it was only a short bus ride away and how it had a very good reputation. 'My son's at university now,' she added proudly.

I could tell that Ben was far more interested in the school than in anything else he had been told all day. In fact, if he'd just been told that Mrs Daniels was an axe-murderer, I reckoned it wouldn't have made any difference to his plans now that he knew there was a really good school here for me to go to.

Ben looked at his watch, then pushed away his plate even though he hadn't finished his baked potato. 'Mr Rutherford must have finished interviewing that other bloke by now,' he said. 'Come on.

Let's go and find out what he's decided. You can bring that sandwich with you.'

Since I'm a picky eater at the best of times, I was only too happy to leave my half-eaten sandwich where it was. The bread was pretty dry in any case. As Ben paid the bill I noticed a plate of scones sitting behind the counter. They looked dry too, as well as being burnt on top, and I found myself wondering if Mrs Daniels hadn't been right after all about the pub food being better. But if we hadn't come in here, we wouldn't have got all this information about her, would we?

And I suddenly thought that maybe the quality of the food wasn't the only thing that had prompted her to suggest we had lunch in the pub.

✻ 6 ✻

'I really can't believe it!' Ben kept saying over and over for the next few days after he found out he'd got the job. All he could talk about was how he didn't want to let Mr Rutherford down. He even used our credit card to buy himself four gardening books, despite the fact that they were expensive. Apparently gardening books had become essentials in our life now.

'You know, I can't figure it out,' Ben said as he handed me one of his new books and asked me to test him on the names of a long list of different types of weed. 'I mean, why give the job to me? That other guy was an experienced gardener – a bit surly, maybe, but then so is everybody else at Thornton Hall. I reckon he'd have fitted in fine there, whereas you and me, with our sunny personalities . . .' He was only half joking, I could tell.

'*I* can do surly,' I replied swiftly.

He laughed. 'I guess that's true.'

We moved into the cottage at Thornton Hall the weekend after Ben's interview. In the space of a week Ben had given notice on our flat, got rid of our own furniture to a local second-hand shop and borrowed a mate's car to transport the rest of our things from the flat to our new home. We had also had to inform my school, say a rapid goodbye to our friends and email Lou with our new address. There had been two emails waiting for us from Lou – one for me and one for Ben – telling us all her news from India. Apparently the food wasn't agreeing with Greg, who had already had a bout of diarrhoea, but she was fine and really enjoying herself.

The day after we moved – the whole thing was so sudden that Ben and I were both feeling like this was just a weekend away rather than a permanent change in our lives – Mrs Daniels came round to drop off some extra bedding and some mousetraps. 'I haven't found any more droppings, but you never know,' she informed us briskly. She wasn't dressed in black this time. She had on a navy skirt and a dark green blouse. She told Ben she would meet him at nine o'clock sharp on Monday morning to show him where all the gardening equipment was kept. 'And then Mr Rutherford wants to show you the grounds himself – and let you know what he expects from you.'

There was one thing I was desperate to know about Thornton Hall – so desperate that I even felt brave enough to ask Mrs Daniels about it. 'Is there a *walled* garden here?' I blurted out as she was about to leave. If there was, then that would make me feel even more like Mary in *The Secret Garden*.

'There's the old sun garden,' she replied crisply. 'It's on the south side of the house, though it's in a dreadful state compared with how it was in my Geoffrey's day.' She looked at Ben. 'That's something else you need to sort out.' She sighed loudly. 'When I think how my late husband toiled over the gardens here . . .'

And that's when Ben made his move. 'Mrs Daniels,' he began earnestly, 'I really want to do a good job here. I really want to make the garden as good as it was when Mr Daniels was alive. I was wondering . . . would you help me by telling me a bit about how *he* did things?'

She looked taken aback and a bit suspicious. 'I thought you'd have your own ideas! You young ones usually do!'

'But *you've* seen the grounds when they were at their best,' he reminded her.

'Well . . . I do have some photographs of how the garden used to be,' she began slowly, in a slightly softer voice. 'And it's true, my husband had a great knowledge of gardening, some of which he did pass on to me. It's like I kept saying to that Jimmy – he was the last boy who came here, who called himself a gardener – there's no substitute for experience when it comes to gardening. It just isn't the sort of thing you can learn from a book.' Her gaze fell on one of Ben's gardening books which was lying on the table – *Gardening for Beginners*. She frowned at it.

'That book's mine,' I said, picking it up.

'I guess we all have to start somewhere, Mrs Daniels,' Ben put in quickly. 'I mean, when your husband started out he must have been new to it all too.'

'Oh yes, but then my Geoffrey was a *born* gardener,' Mrs Daniels said proudly.

I was about to point out that surely you either *needed* experience to be a good gardener or you didn't? And nobody was *born* with gardening experience, were they? But the look Ben gave me when I opened my mouth soon made me close it again.

I said what I thought to Ben as soon as she'd gone though.

'She just meant that her Geoffrey . . .' He grinned. '. . . I mean, her *husband*, had a natural talent for gardening, that's all.'

'Well maybe *you've* got a natural talent too,' I told him. 'Maybe *you're* a born gardener, only you just don't know it yet.'

'I don't think so,' he said. 'I mean, I'm not exactly famous for my horticultural prowess, am I?'

I thought about him killing that plant of Lou's by giving it aspirin and I had to admit that he had a point.

On Monday, just before Ben was due to start work, we had a big row. As there were only two weeks of the summer term left, Ben had already agreed that I could forget about going to a new school until it was time for me to start secondary school after the summer holidays. The row started when he asked what I was going to be doing all day instead.

'Apart from going to social services to tell them I'm home alone, do you mean?' I joked. (Ben had already started worrying that, with Lou gone, I was going to be left in the house on my own too much.)

Ben glared at me like he didn't think that was at all funny.

'Look, I was only joking,' I told him quickly. 'Don't worry! I'll be fine! I'm going to go exploring today, OK?'

And that's when he told me I wasn't to go nosing around Thornton Hall – or its gardens.

'But it's the gardens I want to explore!' I protested. '*Why* can't I?'

'Thornton Hall isn't our house,' Ben reminded me. 'Just because I work in the garden, it doesn't mean it's some sort of playground for *you*.'

'I wasn't going to use it as a playground! Anyway, Mr Rutherford already said I could go on his swing.'

'Only while I was having my interview. If you want swings, you can go to the village. There's a park there.'

'I don't want to go to the village!'

'*Mary, Mary, quite contrary*,' Ben said dismissively. 'That's you today, is it?'

I glared at him. He knows I hate that stupid nursery rhyme. That's another thing I've got in common with Mary in *The Secret Garden*. She hates that rhyme too, because the other kids used to sing it to her in a nasty way when she was all alone and bad-tempered at the start of the story.

'I'll just stay inside and watch TV and get paler and paler then, since you don't seem to care about me getting healthy outside any more!' I snapped. (Unfortunately, thinking about Mary in *The Secret Garden* seems to turn me into her sometimes.) I stomped off into my bedroom and slammed the door.

Ben yelled after me, 'You *do* that, you little drama queen!'

'I am *not* a drama queen!' I screeched back at him.

'You're a little madam who thinks the whole world revolves around her, that's what you are!' I heard him leave the house, banging the front door shut really loudly. Sometimes – especially if he's very stressed out about something – Ben can get in just as bad a mood with me as I'm in with him.

I was so angry I punched my pillow and swore out loud. It wasn't fair! I knew Ben was nervous at the prospect of starting his new job, which was why he was so tense. But I was new here too – with no friends and nothing to do – and I didn't see why I shouldn't go off and explore the gardens if I wanted to.

I reckoned Ben would be tied up for quite a while with Mrs Daniels since she was showing him the gardening equipment in the outbuildings at the back of the house. Apparently there was a big sit-on lawnmower that Ben had to learn how to use today because the grass already needed cutting again. So he wasn't going to see what I did – or where I went – was he?

I put on my trainers and stepped outside. It was a lovely sunny day and straight away I started to pretend that I was Mary in *The Secret Garden* when *she* first goes out into the grounds of the house to go exploring. It's winter then, not summer, and the grounds are cold and bare. That's when she first sees the robin that lives in the garden and it starts to become her friend.

I didn't see any robins as I followed the path that Mrs Daniels had brought us along when she'd first shown us the cottage. After it came out on to the main drive, I walked along it for a bit, then cut across the grass between some trees, heading for the side of the house where the square tower made it look lopsided. Mrs Daniels had said that the walled garden was on the south side of the house. I didn't know which side was south but I guessed it was the opposite side to where I'd gone on the day of Ben's interview, since the garden there had been open and full of rose beds.

A narrow stone path led round to the back of the house, so I followed it. I stopped short when I got to where the outbuildings were, but I couldn't see anybody. I made a run for it, past the old brick sheds and the area where the bins were kept, still following the path, which turned abruptly away from the house and went through a bit of the garden that looked like it hadn't been worked in for a while. I heard the sound of a lawnmower starting up somewhere nearby so I guessed that Ben was already being kept busy.

The path ran alongside a high grey stone wall and after a while I came to the end of it and found an adjoining wall at a right angle. The path split here – one branch carried on straight ahead but the other turned off and ran along the new wall. I followed the second path, starting to feel excited. This wall was much shorter, and by the time I reached the next corner and the next wall I knew I had found what I'd been looking for. Inside these walls there must be a garden.

I was almost too excited to breathe properly as I crept along the third stretch of wall. Would there be a door here? Would it be unlocked? I knew this garden wasn't really a secret like the one in the story – but I could pretend that it was, couldn't I? And if nobody knew I was coming here, then the fact that I *was* would be some sort of secret at least.

I soon came to a black wooden door in the wall. I twisted the handle and found that it turned quite easily. I pushed the door inwards, stepped over a cracked paving stone – and found myself inside.

Straight away I saw that the garden was nothing like the secret garden in my video. That garden was all wild and rambling, with trees and twisting things growing everywhere in a charming, mysterious sort of tangle. This garden had nothing tall in it whatsoever. There were no trees – just grass and flower beds and walls that were partly bare and partly covered in ivy. In one corner there was a small wooden shed. The grass in the centre obviously hadn't been cut in a while and the flower beds looked like they had been left to their own devices for a long time too.

The path was very weedy. It curved round the garden between the overgrown lawn in the middle and the flower beds on the edges, and I followed it all the way round until I got back to the entrance again. The garden wasn't very big really. In the very centre was a stone pillar thing and I went over to look at it. It was a sundial. Its face was brass but in need of a good clean and its stone base had long grass and yellow dandelions growing halfway up it. I remembered now that Mrs Daniels had called this the old sun garden.

'Why isn't anyone looking after you?' I said out loud to the garden. Of course it was probably just because there was no gardener, but then I thought about Mary Lennox's secret garden and how *it* had been locked up and neglected because the wife of the master of the house had fallen out of a tree there and died. It suddenly occurred to me that I didn't know anything about Mr Rutherford's wife. Was it possible that some tragedy had befallen *her* while she was in this garden and that was why it had been left in this state? After all, the rest of the grounds had been kept reasonably tidy, even if they didn't satisfy Mrs Daniels' high standards, whereas the garden inside these walls hadn't been touched all year by the look of it.

There were roses in the flower beds – all yellow ones – and lots of other plants growing in among them, as well as yellow daisies of different types and sizes, and some other yellow flowers that looked a bit like lilies, growing in big clumps. Everything was growing into everything else.

A sort of bindweed with floppy white flowers that I recognized from one of Ben's gardening books was twisting itself around everything. I remembered that the book had given this weed a special name that sounded just right for it – *convolvulus*. 'You're a weed – not a flower,' I told it sternly, 'and you shouldn't be strangling those roses.' I stepped closer and started to tug at some of the bindweed that was choking the yellow rose bush nearest to me.

'Ouch!' I drew back my hand as I got pricked by a rose thorn. I didn't let that stop me though. I went back to the rose, more carefully this time, finding a place where I could break the bindweed easily. I unwound it in both directions from the rose stem, taking care not to touch any of the thorns, and threw the weed on to the path.

I started to imagine that Mary Lennox was with me and that we were working together in the real secret garden. *'Can't you just hear the poor roses sighing with relief as we free them?'* Mary said in her old-fashioned, slightly imperious voice, and I nodded as I replied, *'Now they'll be able to breathe properly again.'* Only I said it in a posh voice too – and all of a sudden I felt like I *was* Mary Lennox.

It took quite a while to free each prickly stem and it wasn't until I glanced at my watch some time later that I realized I'd been working in the garden for nearly an hour. My hands and arms were all scratched because it was difficult to avoid the rose thorns completely, but I didn't care. I was enjoying myself.

'You should wear gardening gloves if you're going to do that!' a voice said from behind me.

And I turned to see – standing grinning at me – the plump boy with the freckled face and curly hair who I had seen that day in the car with Mr Rutherford.

* 7 *

'Hi,' I murmured, not knowing what else to say.

The boy was standing in the doorway, eating a big bar of chocolate and, as I spoke, he stuffed a double chunk into his mouth and started to munch it. His mouth was so full of chocolate that it was a while before he could speak again. 'I know you,' he finally mumbled. 'You were talking to my dad the other day. Your brother's our new gardener, isn't he?'

'Yes,' I said quickly. 'I'm Mary.' And that's when I decided that I wanted to be called Mary by everyone from now on.

'So, are you helping him or something?' he asked, glancing at the pile of weeds I'd left on the path.

'Not exactly,' I said. 'I just really wanted to find this garden.'

'Why?' He looked curious.

'Mrs Daniels told me about it yesterday. This is the walled garden, you see,' I explained lamely.

'I guess it is . . . since it's got walls and it's a garden,' the boy said, smirking.

I scowled with embarrassment – just as fiercely as

Mary Lennox would have done. 'I don't like people making fun of me!'

He just grinned even more. 'That's exactly what Mrs Daniels said to Dad! Didn't you and your brother laugh at her or something when she opened the door to you?'

I felt myself growing hotter. 'We didn't do that on purpose. It's just that—'

But before I could go into any explanation, he interrupted me. 'It's OK. I'm glad you laughed at her. She needs to loosen up a bit. Here . . .' He held out his bar of chocolate to offer me some. 'I'm Alex, by the way.'

I shook my head at the chocolate. I didn't feel like accepting any sort of peace offering from him just yet – if that's what it was meant to be. Besides, his fingers looked sticky and they'd been all over that chocolate. I wished he'd go away so I could go back to my task of unwinding the convolvulus from the roses.

'It's really terrible that this poor garden's been left to get in such a mess,' I said in quite a haughty voice. I was half inclined to ask him if there had been some sort of tragedy here, but I thought I'd better not. After all, if someone *had* fallen out of a tree in this garden and died – not that there were any trees, but maybe Mr Rutherford had had the culprit cut down afterwards – then Alex was highly likely to be related to them, wasn't he?

'Jimmy hardly ever did any work in here, that's why,' Alex explained, sitting down on one of the two wooden benches at the side of the path. 'He was the last gardener here. He was a nice guy, but he was pretty lazy. I think he did cut the lawn in here once

69

– not that you'd know it now. Mostly he just came in here to smoke. Look.' He pointed to some old cigarette butts on the ground by his feet. Jimmy had obviously favoured this bench when he was taking his breaks. 'I used to come in here and sit with him sometimes. He told me some really funny stories! He's got these gossipy aunts who run the tea room in the village and they know the comings and goings of everybody!'

'I've met them,' I said. 'And you're right – they *are* gossipy!'

'So was Jimmy,' Alex said. 'He said he reckoned it ran in the family!' He broke himself off another chunk of chocolate, then held out the rest of the bar to me again. 'Sure you don't want some?'

I looked at it. I do like chocolate and I was in a better mood with him now. The bar was nearly finished, so I knew that this was probably my last chance to take up his offer. 'OK,' I said, going across to join him. 'Thanks.' I sat down beside him on the bench, swinging my feet and prodding with my toes at the grass that was growing up through the cracks in the path. 'Do you live here too then?' I asked him.

'Just in the holidays. Most of the time I live with my mum in London. I'm only staying with Dad for the summer. My school broke up a week ago so I came here then. I go to a private school. We get longer holidays.' He said it as if he thought I might not know anyone who went to a fee-paying school and was therefore unlikely to know that fact.

'So are your mum and dad divorced?' I asked, trying not to feel too disappointed that his mother was clearly alive and therefore not part of some tragic, romantic story involving the garden after all.

'Yeah. My brother and me always spend the holidays with Dad. We came here for Easter just after Dad moved in. That was cool. But now Christopher's gone off on holiday with his mates so I'm stuck here on my own for the whole summer.'

'My big sister's just gone off travelling too,' I said sympathetically. 'She's gone to India.'

'Chris has gone to Italy. He's going to do loads of painting there. He's a brilliant artist. I reckon he's going to be really famous one day. He's going to art college after the summer. It's in London, which means he gets to stay at home, so that's good! I think I'd really miss him if he went away anywhere.'

I thought about Lou and bit my lip. 'How old is he?' I asked.

'Eighteen. I'm twelve. How old are you?'

'Eleven and a half,' I told him. 'You've only just had your birthday, haven't you? I know because your dad showed me your birthday cake when I met him that time on the train. I saved it from being sat on. Did he tell you about that?'

He nodded. 'He doesn't usually get me a birthday cake. He only did this year because I had to stay with him that weekend because Mum was away on business. I was pretty annoyed with her for going away on my birthday actually.'

'But did you like the cake?' I asked.

'Yeah – but Dad and I had a big argument about it afterwards.'

'An argument?' I was puzzled. 'Why?'

'Dad reckoned I shouldn't have eaten it so quickly!'

'Why? How quickly *did* you eat it?'

'In three days! I finished it off the day after I took it home with me and Mum went and told him. The next time Dad spoke to me on the phone he said I was greedy, so then we argued really badly and I was so angry I threw the wings away.'

'The aeroplane wings?'

He nodded. 'See, they weren't just there to decorate the cake – they were part of a model aeroplane kit Dad got me as a birthday present. Not that I wanted a model kit. I hate the idea of sitting putting all those fiddly bits together – it's really nerdy, if you ask me. But Dad never thinks about what *I* want. He thinks all boys should either be outside playing healthy games in the fresh air, or inside doing things that improve their minds – like making models.' He pulled a pained face as he spoke. '*He* used to spend hours making model planes when he was my age, so he says . . . Anyway, he wasn't very pleased when I told him that unfortunately I *couldn't* make this particular model plane because the wings had already been taken away by the binmen.'

'I can imagine,' I said, staring at him with something like awe. I didn't like to think about what Ben would say if he'd spent loads of money on a birthday present for me and I'd chucked half of it away.

Suddenly the garden door swung open and Ben walked in. He did a double take when he saw me. He was red-faced and sweaty-looking and he had grass cuttings on his shirt and in his hair. 'What are *you* doing here?' he asked me crossly.

I quickly pointed at Alex. 'It's his garden. He says I can be here.'

Mr Rutherford walked in through the gate behind

Ben. His eyes fell first on me, then on Alex and finally on the remains of the large chocolate bar in Alex's hand. He looked irritated. 'Alex, you've only just had your breakfast.' It was very clear that he was about to say more to his son, whose face had instantly become redder and more defiant-looking.

But before he could speak again, I snatched the chocolate out of Alex's hand and said quickly, 'I bought myself some chocolate, Ben – I was just giving Alex a bit. You know how you're always going on at me to drink more milk? Well this has got a pint and a half of full-cream milk in it! It says so on the label.' (Ben had recently decided that I had to drink plenty of milk every day, because he reckons it's good for you. Since I hate milk, we'd been arguing about it quite a lot.)

Alex looked so surprised that I was afraid his father would guess straight away that I was lying, but fortunately Mr Rutherford wasn't looking at him. He was looking at me – not bothering to mask the fact that he thought I was quite a strange child. (Unfortunately, Ben was looking at me too – not bothering to hide the fact that *he* thought I was making fun of his new milk rule and that, when he got me home, he was going to make me drink a pint and a half of the stuff in our fridge.)

'Well . . . you two have met each other then,' Mr Rutherford grunted. 'That's good.' He turned away from Alex and me to look at my brother. 'This is the walled garden I was telling you about, Ben. Mrs Daniels tells me it shouldn't be difficult to get it into shape in time.'

'In time for *what*?' I asked curiously.

'For the competition,' Mr Rutherford said, turning

back to face me. He explained that Lower Thornton and all the neighbouring villages held a garden open day on the first weekend in August every year. 'All the local houses who want to take part open up their gardens for the public to view. There are several competitions and one of them is for the best small garden. Mrs Daniels suggested that since we've got a proper gardener now, we might as well enter. What do you think, Ben?'

Ben was scowling at the garden as if he would dearly love to give it – and Mrs Daniels herself – a large dose of aspirin. 'I don't know,' he mumbled gruffly.

'You don't know *what*?'

'I don't know if it's going to be ready four weeks from now,' Ben answered in a tight voice.

Ben looked like he was being slowly strangled by bindweed himself and I had a horrible feeling that this news, added to whatever other gardening horrors he had already encountered today, might be enough to make him crack completely. And if he cracked, he might blurt out to Mr Rutherford that he had never gardened before in his life, and then we would have to leave Thornton Hall.

Suddenly I had an idea.

'Can *I* have this garden to look after?' I asked. 'I'd really like to have something special to do here. I could make this garden win that competition – I know I could!'

Mr Rutherford, Ben and Alex all stared at me.

'Please?' I begged. And suddenly I thought of something else that made the whole idea seem even more exciting. 'I can make it my very own *secret* garden until I'm ready to show it to everyone. I can lock the door so no one can come in until it's finished.'

'May, this isn't make-believe,' Ben said impatiently. He looked at Mr Rutherford apologetically. 'She's got this video about a girl who finds a secret garden. She thinks it'd be like that.'

'Are you talking about *The Secret Garden* by Frances Hodgson Burnett?' Mr Rutherford asked, looking at me with renewed interest.

I nodded. (I recognized the name of the author who'd written the original book because it always appeared on the TV screen along with the title while the oboe music was playing at the beginning.)

'She must've watched that video about a hundred times,' Ben added.

'You should read the book,' Mr Rutherford told me. 'I think you'd enjoy it.'

'She might not enjoy it as much as watching it on TV though,' Alex said in a challenging voice. He was looking at his father as he spoke, as if he was deliberately having a dig at him about something.

Whatever it was, Mr Rutherford ignored him and continued briskly, 'Mary, I admire your enthusiasm, but this garden would be far too much work for you to do on your own. Unless . . .' He suddenly looked at Alex, as if an idea had just come to him. 'Unless you were to help her, Alex. Then the two of you could do it together.'

'Oh yes!' I gasped. 'That's a brilliant idea!' I grasped Alex's arm excitedly. 'Then it'd be even more like *The Secret Garden*! Mary had a boy friend who helped *her*.'

'A boyfriend?' Alex looked alarmed.

I felt myself blushing as I said quickly, 'I mean, a

friend who was a boy. Oh, please say you'll do it, Alex. It'll be cool.'

I could tell Alex was torn between wanting to have some fun with me and *not* wanting to please his father too much, but finally he nodded his agreement. 'OK.'

'Good!' Mr Rutherford smiled warmly at both of us before turning to Ben, who had been watching all this with a dazed expression. 'Well, Ben, it looks like you're off the hook as far as *this* garden goes. But I'm sure you can find plenty of other work to keep you busy, can't you? If you need any help with anything, Mrs Daniels is the person to ask. She knows a surprising amount about gardening.'

'So I've gathered,' Ben said.

'Dad, we're going to need some money if we're going to buy new plants and stuff,' Alex put in suddenly.

'When we've cleared some space, we could plant some seeds,' I suggested. 'Seeds aren't expensive.'

'It's too late to grow anything from seed now,' Ben informed us. 'And even if you bought annuals as bedding plants and watered them in, they wouldn't be ready in time for the competition.'

'What's an annual?' Alex asked my brother, and for an awful moment I thought Ben was going to be exposed as a fraud, right there in front of Mr Rutherford. But I needn't have worried. Apparently that was quite an easy question if you'd read a few gardening books. 'It's a plant that only flowers once – it doesn't come back the following year like perennials do,' Ben explained.

'I think you should concentrate on sorting out

what's already here, don't you?' Alex's father said, looking around at the overcrowded flower beds.

'OK,' I agreed, going over to the garden door to inspect the keyhole. The most important thing to me was that this was a *secret* garden and it could only be that if we were able to lock it. 'But we need to find the key first.'

Alex came over to inspect the door too. 'Do *you* know where the key is, Dad?' he asked.

'I imagine if it's anywhere, it'll be in the cupboard in the kitchen passage – the one opposite the laundry room. That's where all the keys were kept when your great-aunt lived here. But you and Mary had better ask Mrs Daniels about it.'

'Come on, Mary. Let's go and ask her now!' Alex said.

'Since when have you started calling yourself Mary?' Ben suddenly asked me. 'I thought you only liked May.'

'Well, now I like Mary better,' I said firmly. 'And I want *you* to call me Mary too from now on, because that's my proper name.'

He gave a little grunt and murmured, 'Whatever . . .' but somehow he didn't sound like he was planning on busting a gut trying to remember.

'Is it OK if I go with Alex now?' I added, thinking that I ought to at least make a show of asking his permission before heading off, especially since I'd already disobeyed him once today by coming here when he'd told me not to.

'So long as it's OK with Mr Rutherford,' Ben replied. 'It's his house.'

'Of course it's all right with me!' Mr Rutherford's eyes seemed almost twinkly as he added, 'I'm delighted that Alex has found someone his own age to keep him company this summer.' And for a fleeting moment I wondered if he had employed Ben rather than that other, more experienced gardener just because Ben came with a ready-made friend for his son.

* 8 *

It was the second time I had been inside the house. The first time had been on the day of Ben's interview, when we'd been invited into the library on our return after lunch to find out whether or not Ben had got the job. But on that day we'd entered through the front door whereas this time Alex showed me in through a side door and I found myself in a corridor with a stone floor that led to some steps further ahead.

'That's the old laundry,' Alex said, pointing to a door on the left. 'This is the cupboard Dad was talking about.' He opened a door on the right to reveal a walk-in cupboard. He switched on a dim light and stepped inside. The cupboard looked like it was mainly used to house things that were no longer needed. There was an old-fashioned hoover, a couple of ancient heaters and some rolls of carpet sitting on the floor. The shelves were full of cardboard boxes with things stuffed into them. Poking out of the top of the nearest box were some rusty saucepans, another was filled with chipped crockery and lined up along one shelf were some dusty oil lamps. There were some wellington boots piled up in one corner, along with an assortment of umbrellas, half of them twisted-looking and broken.

On one wall of the cupboard was a board with hooks on it. Bunches of keys were dangling from the hooks, some of them tagged with faded paper labels. Alex was inspecting all the keys, reading the various labels. 'Outhouse 1, Outhouse 2, Side door, Conservatory, Attic, Cellars . . . Those are all the ones with labels.'

'The garden key should be a very old one,' I said. 'And bigger than these, I reckon.'

'We'd better ask Mrs Daniels if she knows where it is,' he said.

He led me up the steps into a small hall, off which there were two more closed doors and a staircase leading upwards. Straight ahead was the main passageway leading into the bulk of the house, and to our right was a narrower passageway, which Alex told me led to the family living room, his father's study and the conservatory.

'That's the breakfast room and that's the staircase to the cellars,' Alex explained, pointing to the two closed doors in turn. 'The breakfast room leads into the kitchen. Mrs Daniels might be in there.' He led me into a nice light room with a large oak table in the middle and big windows that looked out on to the back terrace and gardens. 'We eat all our meals in here,' he said. 'Not just breakfast.' The room was linked to the kitchen but Mrs Daniels wasn't there. Alex led me through the kitchen door and out into the corridor again. 'That's the dining room,' he said, pointing to a door opposite the kitchen one. 'It's really posh. We never use it. Do you want to see?'

I nodded so he led me into the room, which was

huge and very grand indeed. It had a polished wooden floor with a big red patterned rug covering the main part of it, and there was a highly polished mahogany table in the centre with eight finely-carved chairs set around it. There was also a huge marble fireplace with a white marble bust of some Greek goddess sitting at one end and a large blue vase at the other, which Alex told me was made of Venetian glass and had been brought back from Italy by his great-aunt fifty years ago. The room had three big windows to the front of the house and another door at the far side.

'This is the grandest house I've ever been in,' I told Alex.

'Do you want to see the rest of it?' he asked.

I nodded. 'But remember, we've got to find Mrs Daniels too.' Alex strode across the room, saying, 'Excuse us, madame,' in a mock-deferential tone to the white marble head as he passed it. He opened the other door and we were in the main hall, which I recognized from the day of Ben's interview. The room on the right as you entered the house was the living room I had seen that day when I'd looked in through the window. Ahead of us was the rear hall with the library off it. It had an ornate wooden stair-case leading upwards in a sort of arc.

I paused outside the door to the library, because I knew from my previous visit that there was a computer in there. 'Are you on the Internet here?' I asked Alex.

'Yeah. Why?'

'Do you think your dad would mind if I emailed my sister?'

'We'll need to ask him. He's got this rule about me

not going online without his permission.' He led me up the staircase to a landing where three large bright modern pictures were hanging on the wall. 'My brother painted those,' Alex said proudly. 'Dad took down the gloomy old portraits my great-aunt had up there.'

'Is your brother into *modern* art then?' I asked, taking in the large colourful shapes which were quite striking to look at but which didn't seem to represent any real objects as far as I could make out.

Alex nodded. 'He does more traditional stuff too, but that's the kind of painting he likes doing best.'

'I think I like more normal pictures myself,' I said. 'You know – when you can actually tell what it is.'

Alex laughed again. 'I'll show you some of his other stuff if you like.' We were standing at one end of the long upper-floor landing and he showed me into a small room which he told me his brother had used as a studio when they'd stayed there at Easter. 'There are twelve bedrooms in total, so Dad said Chris could have this one to work in,' Alex said, pointing to some large blank canvases leaning up against one wall. 'Dad bought those for him as a surprise because he thought he'd be coming here this summer.'

But my attention had been caught by something else. 'Did your brother do these?' I asked, pointing to a pile of sketches lying on top of an old chest of drawers.

'Yeah.'

I picked them up to study them better. There were drawings of the house from several different angles and some sketches of people, one of which was clearly Mr Rutherford.

'He did a drawing of me too,' Alex said. 'Dad got it framed. It's hanging in my room, if you want to see it.'

He led me further along the corridor past two or three closed doors before stopping at one on the left which had a sticker on the outside saying: PRIVATE: KEEP OUT!

He opened the door and walked in. The room had an old-fashioned wardrobe and chest of drawers, a single bed with a Bart Simpson duvet cover and a large square rug on the floor that looked like a snakes-and-ladders board. 'Dad chose that,' Alex said, seeing me looking at the rug. 'I hate board games.' There were two windows overlooking the front grounds and between them was a table piled up with comics and a chair with a cushion on it.

'It's very tidy,' I said. 'Much tidier than my bedroom is.' Although, since I had stopped sharing with my sister, my own room was a lot tidier than it used to be. Ben had noticed that too and had made a wry comment the other day about how he could see now that it wasn't me who had been the messy one.

'Yeah, well, there's not much to keep tidy – most of my stuff is back in London,' Alex replied.

On the wall above Alex's bed there was a framed sketch in bold pencil of Alex's head and shoulders. 'It's brilliant,' I said. 'It looks just like you!'

'He said he'd do a proper painting of me this summer. That was before he decided to go off to Italy instead.'

'Is this his too?' I asked, picking up a sketch pad that was lying on Alex's bedside table. I started to flick through it. The first three pages were half-finished sketches of the view from Alex's window. I

83

was about to turn over to the next page when he snatched the pad away from me.

'What's wrong?' I asked, looking at him in surprise.

'Nothing.' His face had gone tense all of a sudden. 'Come on. We still have to find Mrs Daniels.'

I was curious about what it was he didn't want me to see, but there was no time to ask any more because he was already leading me out of the room.

At the far end of the house there were several spare bedrooms, and at the end of the landing was the other staircase, which descended to the small back hall we had passed through downstairs. Another short corridor led off from here, at a right angle to the main landing.

'This is where Mrs Daniels' rooms are,' Alex said, leading me along the corridor. I guessed we were now in the bit of the house that jutted forwards and which made the house look uneven when you saw it from the outside. 'That's her bathroom and that's her bedroom,' Alex said, pointing to two doors on our right. 'This one is her sitting room.' We had come to the end of the corridor and Alex was knocking on a door straight ahead.

'Where does that one go to?' I asked, pointing to a door on the left which he had ignored.

'Oh, that's the door to the tower room. It's locked because nobody's allowed to go up there. The floor's rotten so it's too dangerous until it gets repaired.' He was pushing open the door to Mrs Daniels' sitting room, calling out her name. I followed him into the room curiously, taking in the chintz-covered sofa, the small fireplace with the mirror above it, the bookshelves filled with old paperbacks and the sewing machine on the table in the corner. There was no sign of the housekeeper.

'Maybe she's having a lie-down,' I suggested as we stepped back out on to the landing.

'She never lies down – she's always working during the day,' Alex said, knocking on her bedroom and bathroom doors as we passed them, but receiving no response. 'I suppose she must have gone out to the shops or something.'

But as we retreated to the end of the corridor and started to walk back along the main landing, we heard a noise behind us like a door closing. We looked at each other.

'Come on.' Alex led the way back to Mrs Daniels' corridor, where we found her standing facing us at the far end, holding a tray.

'What are you doing here?' she snapped.

'We were looking for you,' Alex replied. 'Where *were* you just now?'

'In my sitting room, having a rest!' she replied sharply. 'Now, what do you want?'

'But—' Alex broke off, clearly thinking better of telling her we had already been inside her sitting room. 'Dad thought that you might know where the key to the garden is . . . the walled garden.'

She stared at him blankly for a moment, then started briskly towards us with the tray. 'Here.' She handed it to Alex. 'Take this down to the kitchen. I'll come in a minute.'

Alex and I looked at each other again. I knew we were both thinking the same thing. Why had she lied about being in her sitting room just now? And where had she really been? We were halfway down the stairs when my curiosity suddenly got the better of me. 'I'm going back to see what she's doing,' I whispered. Alex remained where he was as I tiptoed back upstairs and peered round the corner into Mrs Daniels' corridor. The housekeeper was standing outside the door that Alex had said led to the tower room. She was locking it with a key.

I went back quickly to rejoin Alex. 'She's locking the door to the tower room,' I whispered to him. 'That must be where she came from just now!'

We could hear her footsteps moving along the corridor.

'Quick – before she sees us!' Alex led the way down the remainder of the stairs, but thankfully Mrs Daniels didn't immediately follow.

'Why do you think she lied about where she was?' I asked Alex when we had reached the safety of the kitchen and closed the door behind us.

'I don't know,' Alex said. 'She knows no one's allowed in the tower room. Maybe she's afraid we'll tell Dad.'

'But what do you think she was doing up there?' I was looking at the tray that he had just put down next to the sink. It held a flowery tea plate with crumbs on it, a dirty cup and saucer, a small teapot and an empty milk jug. 'What if the floor isn't rotten at all in the tower room?' I suggested. 'What if Mrs Daniels just told your father that to stop anyone from going up there?'

'Why would she do that?' Alex asked.

'What if she's got someone hidden up there?' I was thinking about a film I had watched on TV one Sunday afternoon with Louise. It was called *Jane Eyre* and in that story the housekeeper was helping to keep a mad person hidden away at the top of the house.

'Don't be stupid!' Alex replied. 'She'll just have been up there fetching something, I expect.'

'Maybe . . . or maybe she's got some mad relative we don't know about and that's who she's keeping up there.' I was starting to feel quite excited.

'*You're* the one who's mad!' Alex said, looking at me in disbelief. 'Look, let's just *ask* her what she was doing in the tower room, OK?'

'No way!' I gasped, horrified.

'Why not?' he demanded.

'Because if Mrs Daniels finds out we saw her, you don't know what she might do to stop us giving away her secret,' I answered. I was thinking of the sinister housekeeper in *Rebecca*, who becomes totally murderous by the end of the film.

Alex looked amused. 'You like secrets a lot, don't you, Mary?'

I narrowed my eyes. 'What's that supposed to mean?'

He shook his head, grinning. 'Nothing.'

The kitchen door opened before I could say anything else. As Mrs Daniels entered, I noticed she was carrying a big bunch of keys – one of which must be the key to the tower room.

'Now,' she said briskly, looking at Alex, 'what was it you wanted?'

'The key to the walled garden,' Alex answered quickly. 'Do you know where it is?'

She shook her head. 'The sun garden has never been locked. I don't think there *is* a key.'

'The sun garden?' Alex queried. I hadn't told him about Mrs Daniels calling it that, I realized now.

'That's what my husband always called the walled garden, because of the sundial in the middle. And because he planted nothing but yellow flowers there.'

'I *wondered* why all the flowers were yellow,' I said, forgetting about everything but the garden for a moment. 'What a lovely idea – to make a completely yellow garden!'

She looked at me then. 'He and I used to sit there in the summer evenings sometimes, enjoying all the scents, and Geoffrey used to say that his roses were glowing in the sun. Those flower beds were a mass of yellow then.' She paused. 'Of course, they'll need a lot of work to get them back into any kind of shape again. I hope your brother's going to see to that.'

'Mary and I are going to do it,' Alex said. 'But we need to find the key first. We've already looked in the cupboard across from the laundry room and it's not there.'

'There's never been a key to that garden in all the time I've been here,' Mrs Daniels said impatiently. 'What do you want to lock the garden for, anyway? And what do you mean – Mary and you are going to do it?'

'Dad says the two of us can have it as our very own gardening project,' Alex explained, 'but Mary wants to make it a secret garden, don't you, Mary? Except if there isn't a key, I suppose we can't do that.'

I wasn't giving in that easily though. I felt a stubborn Mary Lennox look spreading across my face as I hissed, 'There *is* a key! I know there is! We'll just have to keep looking for it. There must be lots of places in the house where it could be.'

'Never you mind turning this house upside down, young lady,' Mrs Daniels told me swiftly. 'There are parts of this house that are too dangerous for children to go poking about in.'

'You mean, like the tower room?' I retorted just as swiftly.

Mrs Daniels gave me a cool look. 'That's right. The floor in the tower room certainly isn't safe.' She paused for a few moments before adding, 'And neither are the cellars. A nosy child could easily get shut in those cellars and nobody would ever know. That's why I always keep the door locked – to prevent mishaps like that.'

And from the way she was looking at me, I got the feeling that if I accidently got locked in the cellars, it was highly likely that she wouldn't be able to find *that* key either.

❋ 9 ❋

'Dad, can Mary email her sister?' Alex asked.

Mr Rutherford was showing Ben some piece of machinery in one of the outhouses and they both turned round as Alex and I appeared at the door.

'May, we'll do that at the local library or an Internet cafe or something,' Ben said quickly. 'You don't need to bother Mr Rutherford.'

'I don't think you'll find many Internet cafes in Lower Thornton,' Mr Rutherford replied before I could. 'And I really don't mind Mary using our computer.'

Ben was shaking his head. 'Thanks, but it's OK.' He turned back to me. 'I need to email Lou too. We'll go and find a public library later.'

'*When* later?' I demanded. Because now that I had got myself all psyched up to email my sister, I wanted to do it immediately.

'You can use our computer too, Ben,' Mr Rutherford said. 'In fact, why don't you go and do it now? We've finished here and it's time you had a break.'

'You need to give us your password for us to log on, Dad,' Alex reminded him.

'I'll come and put it in for you,' his father replied.

He didn't even wait for Ben to agree, but ushered him briskly out of the outhouse before leading us all through the side entrance into the house.

He stopped on his way past the kitchen to tell Mrs Daniels what we were doing. He probably thought that if he didn't, she'd find Ben and me in the library on our own and accuse us of trespassing or something. She came out to tell Ben to take off his gardening boots before going any further – which he did – and she made Alex and me show her the soles of our shoes to check they weren't muddy. She looked at Mr Rutherford's shoes as if she'd like to check those too only she didn't quite dare to ask. Ben was in his socks as we carried on through to the library and he looked a bit embarrassed, which I guessed was because one of his socks had a big hole in it.

Mr Rutherford set us up on the computer, then suggested to Alex, 'Why don't you give your mum a ring while Mary and Ben email their sister? You haven't spoken to her all week.'

So Alex went off to use the other phone line in the family living room, leaving Ben and me alone. Ben was so busy looking round the room admiring all the books that I reckon he'd momentarily forgotten why we were there.

'Wouldn't it be great to actually own a place like this?' he murmured.

'What? This house, you mean?'

'This library!' His eyes were all lit up in a way I hadn't seen since he'd entered a competition in a magazine last year and nearly won the prize. You'd had to write an article on ancient Greece or something, and the prize had been to have your article published and to go on a trip to visit some ruins in

Athens. It wasn't my idea of a fun holiday, but Ben had been ecstatic when he'd got the letter telling him he'd been shortlisted. In the end he'd only been a runner-up and he'd been so disappointed when he found out that he'd actually cried. Like I already said, Ben never cries in front of us – and he only did it then for about five seconds before rushing off to his bedroom and slamming the door.

'Let's see if Lou's sent *us* anything first,' Ben said now, coming over to help me access my in-box.

Lou had sent me an email and I shooed Ben away from the computer so I could read it in private.

Hi, May-flower

(Lou hadn't called me that since I was little.)

I am having the most amazing time here, but I'm really missing you. Greg and I both have the runs now but we're doing loads of fantastic things when we're not on the loo!!! There are some beautiful temples here and I wish you could see them too! (She described the temple she had visited the day before and went on to tell me a funny story about one of the other backpackers they had met there.) *I must stop now and write an email to Ben as well. Write back soon and tell me what you've been doing. What is the cottage like? Have you found any secret gardens yet?!*

She put her name after that, and about twenty kisses.

'I know she hasn't even been gone two weeks,' I said gloomily, after I'd finished reading it, 'but it feels like much longer than that to me.'

'Well . . . a lot's happened since she left,' Ben replied.

'I wonder what it's going to feel like when we haven't seen her for a whole *year*,' I went on. 'Like we haven't seen her for a *hundred* years, probably.'

'Or maybe it won't feel any worse than it feels now,' Ben suggested. 'Maybe once you *know* you're not going to see someone again for a whole year, you just start missing them as much as you're going to, straight away.'

'Do you think?' I asked hopefully. It was a comforting thought that I might not be going to feel any worse than I already did about Lou being gone. But I knew Ben might just be saying that to make me feel better.

'I guess we'll find out, won't we?' he said.

'Can I write my reply now, or do you want to read the email she's written to you first?' I asked him.

'You go ahead. I'll read mine when you're done. I'm going to have a nose at some of these books.' Ben crooked his head to one side so that he could read along the book spines while I settled down to compose my message back to Louise.

The first thing I told her about was the walled garden – and how it *was* going to be a secret garden if we could only find the key. Next I told her about Alex and his dad. Then, because I knew how much she'd liked the film of *Rebecca*, I told her that Mrs Daniels was seeming more and more like Mrs Danvers every day. I told her that, despite what the gossipy ladies in the tea room had told us, nothing mysterious had happened in our cottage since we'd moved in and we hadn't seen any mice yet either, thank goodness! Lastly – because I liked saving the best bit till last – I told her about the tower room that was locked up and how Alex and I had caught Mrs Daniels coming down from it with a tray. *I haven't told Ben though! It's TOP SECRET!!! The only people who know about it are Alex, me and you!* I liked the idea of my sister sharing our secret even though she was in India.

As I was signing off – adding even more kisses than she had sent me – the door opened and Mr Rutherford walked in. 'Alex has a kite that we're going to try to fly. He wants to know if you want to come too, Mary.'

'Oh yes, please!' I said, clicking the SEND button on the email. 'I can, can't I, Ben?'

Ben had taken a book from the shelf and was sitting at the table with it. 'Sure,' he said. Mr Rutherford was walking over to see what Ben was reading and my brother quickly shut the book, looking embarrassed. 'I hope you don't mind but I was just having a look at this while—'

'Don't apologize,' Mr Rutherford interrupted him. 'I'm glad to see you're still interested in history. You're welcome to borrow the book if you want.'

'Really?'

'Yes. Let me know what you think about it afterwards.' He looked at me. 'Now . . . if you're ready, Mary . . .'

'Is it all right if I stay here for another ten minutes and write a quick email to my sister?' Ben asked. 'Then I'll get straight back to work.'

Mr Rutherford nodded. 'That's fine. Oh, and Mrs Daniels wants a word with you when you get a minute.'

Ben instantly looked wary. 'What about?'

'I think she's worried about the rose garden.'

'I haven't touched the rose garden!' Ben answered indignantly.

Mr Rutherford looked amused. 'I know. But I

think she wants to give you some advice about it before you do.'

I had a really good time that afternoon. We took a packed lunch with us, which we ate on top of the hill where Alex's father had taken us to fly the kite. It was a bit like having a proper brother to hang out with, I thought, as I ran after Alex across the grass. Because even though I wasn't technically an only child, the age difference between Ben and Louise and me made me feel like I sort of was.

'This kite was a birthday present from Dad too,' Alex told me as we flopped down on the grass together to have a rest. Mr Rutherford was lying on the bank with his eyes closed a short distance away, safely out of earshot. 'It's pretty cool actually, though it wasn't what I really wanted for my birthday.'

'What *did* you really want?' I asked him.

'A TV set.'

'A portable one for your bedroom, you mean?'

'I mean, any kind of one, anywhere in Dad's house! Dad doesn't have one at all. Even my great-aunt – and she was a real old misery guts – even *she* had a TV when Thornton Hall belonged to her. But as soon as Dad moved in he got rid of it and made this really huge thing of declaring the house a TV-free zone.'

'But why?' I was puzzled. I'd never known anyone who objected to living in the same house as a television before.

'He just really disapproves of TV! He says it stunts the imagination and makes people physically and mentally lazy. If you get him on the subject he'll go on for ever. Christopher says it's not worth arguing with him, seeing as how we only ever have to spend the holidays here, but that's all right for him because all he wants to do is paint and Dad buys him all this expensive painting stuff.'

'I watch TV and *I'm* not lazy,' I said, frowning. 'And Lou says I've got a really *active* imagination.' (*Too* active an imagination was what Lou had said when I'd been outlining, in gruesome detail, all the Indiana Jones-style catastrophes that might befall her if she went off travelling with Greg.)

'Who's Lou?' Alex asked.

'My big sister. The one who's in India with her boyfriend.' And I proceeded to describe Greg in less than flattering terms. (Unfortunately, my ability to feel understanding about Lou going away seemed to be diminishing in proportion to the length of time she'd been gone.)

'Dad says you've always lived with your big brother and sister,' Alex said, plucking at the grass as he spoke. 'Haven't you got a mum *or* a dad then?'

'No.'

'How come?' He sounded curious.

'My mum's dead and I've never had a dad.'

He looked thoughtful as he twisted a long blade of grass round his finger. 'Well, *I've* got a mum *and* a dad, so I suppose I'm lucky compared to you – even if they *do* both prefer my big brother to me.'

'How come?' I was the one who was curious now.

'Oh, just because he's so clever and handsome and talented – everything I'm not.'

'He sounds like a pain!'

Alex laughed. 'He's not though. That's the thing – he's dead cool. Even *I* really like him! He has this way of making everything OK when he's around –

like if Dad and me are arguing, he'll always say something that makes us both laugh so that we stop.' He lowered his voice, glancing across to check his father was still snoozing. 'Dad and me *really* don't seem to be getting on with each other now that Chris isn't here. I mean, I sometimes think Dad really *dislikes* me for being here when Chris isn't.'

'Don't be silly!' I protested.

He frowned. 'But it's as if he's really *focusing* on me now that Chris isn't here and noticing all the stuff he doesn't like about me or something.'

'But he went to loads of trouble to get you that birthday cake,' I reminded him. 'Surely he wouldn't have done that if he didn't like you?' I remembered how protective Mr Rutherford had been of that cake on the train and how grateful he had been to me for saving it.

'My birthday was before I came to stay with him for the whole summer,' Alex pointed out. 'He makes this big effort if he's only seeing me for the weekend, but we fall out pretty quickly if we have to spend any longer together than that. This summer I didn't feel like making any effort at all right from the start, because I was in such a bad mood about the television.' He frowned again. 'I just really *miss* it when I come to stay with him, you know? There are all these programmes I always watch and they're like . . . like . . .'

'Like your friends?' I suggested.

'Exactly!' He nodded as if he was really relieved that I understood. 'And now I'm missing them all!'

'Can't your mum tape them for you?'

He shook his head. 'She says there's too much to tape.'

'Well, have you told your dad how you feel about

it?' I asked, because Lou is always saying that when you're upset with someone it usually helps to voice it rather than bottle it up. (Ben is always saying that he wouldn't mind if Lou *did* bottle things up a bit more, but still . . .)

'I've told him, but he won't listen. He says most of what's on TV is rubbish anyway and that I'd be much better off reading a good book. And the other day he said that one of the reasons there are so many overweight children these days is because they watch too much TV and aren't getting enough exercise.'

'That's stupid,' I said immediately. 'If you sit reading a book all day, you're not getting any exercise either, are you?'

Alex nodded. 'Try telling Dad that! He's got an answer for everything. He'd probably say that at least if you were reading a book you'd be exercising your brain cells.'

I looked at Alex, thinking that he *was* pretty plump, but I really didn't see how anyone could blame the television for that. After all, I watched plenty of TV and I'm really skinny. I reckoned that, in Alex's case, being plump probably had more to do with eating large quantities of chocolate. 'Maybe your dad only goes on at you about exercise because he's worried about your arteries or something,' I said. 'If you eat a lot of fat and don't do enough exercise, they get all clogged up. I saw this programme on TV that showed how people get fat in their blood vessels and how it leads to heart disease.'

'Yeah, well, I wouldn't know about that, since I'm not allowed to watch TV,' he replied drily.

I laughed. 'Tell you what – you can come and watch *our* telly if you like.'

'Can I?' He instantly looked more cheerful. 'That'd be great – but we'd need to keep it a secret from Dad.'

I nodded happily. 'I'm good with secrets,' I said.

Mr Rutherford stood up at that point, brushing the grass off his clothes as he came over to join us. 'Well,' he said, 'I guess we should go. This has been fun, though, hasn't it? Good exercise too!'

Alex gave me a look that said, *See what I mean?*

'We should do this again, Alex. What do you think?' his father added.

'Sure,' Alex replied. 'If Mary can come too.'

'Of course she can.' Mr Rutherford looked pleased and I suddenly knew that whatever all this stuff with the television was about, he definitely didn't dislike his son. Because if he disliked Alex, he wouldn't care so much about what he did or didn't do.

That evening, as I told Ben about my afternoon out, he looked pleased too. 'This move has been a good thing for you, hasn't it?' he said.

I nodded. 'What about you?' I asked, because he had seemed totally wrecked when he'd got back to the cottage late this afternoon after his first day at work here. And he'd spent so long soaking his tired muscles in the bath that I'd ended up banging on the door, demanding to know if he'd accidently fallen asleep and drowned.

'I like it too – apart from the gardening!' I knew he was joking, but at the same time I knew it was the sort of joke you make when you're trying to make light of how much you genuinely dislike something. Ben had already started reading the history book that Mr Rutherford had lent him, and I could tell that he was far more interested in learning about medieval England than he was in learning any new gardening skills.

'What did Mrs Daniels say to you about the roses?' I asked him.

He pulled a face. 'Apparently the rose garden was Geoffrey's pride and joy. And guess what? Nobody prunes roses like her Geoffrey pruned them!'

I giggled. 'That figures.'

'She wanted to know what my own pruning technique was.'

'Really? What did you say?'

'The only thing I could remember from all those books I read. I told her my technique was just the same as everyone else's – the weaker the plant, the harder I pruned it. Then I looked at her as if I *could* give her a lecture on the subject but I didn't have time to.'

'So she didn't guess you were bluffing?'

'She didn't seem to.'

'Did you get all of the lawn cut?'

'Most of it. The grounds here are huge. I've got to trim all the edges tomorrow.' He sighed. 'I'd rather not think about that right now.' He got up and went through to the kitchen to start preparing our tea.

'It was nice of Mr Rutherford to let us use his computer, wasn't it?' I said, following him. 'And to lend you that book.'

He nodded, reaching into the cupboard for a jar of pasta sauce. 'He's an OK guy behind all that sternness, I reckon.'

'Alex doesn't think so, though,' I said, taking the

jar from him to check the contents. 'Yuck! This has got mushrooms in it!'

'Has it really?' Ben said coolly, taking the jar back to open it. (He won't negotiate with me any more when it comes to pasta sauces, because he says I'd kick up a fuss no matter what kind he chose.) 'What does Alex say about his dad then?' he asked, sounding interested. But before I could answer he continued, 'I reckon he'd be all right as a dad. I mean, he'd take a bit of an interest at least. You know . . .' He stopped what he was doing and said, '. . . like that man and his son who were sitting behind me on the bus that time – was it Lou I was telling before or you . . . ?'

'Not me,' I said, because this was the first I'd heard of him meeting a father and son on a bus.

'I think it was Lou . . . Anyway, this man and his teenage son were sitting behind me on the bus one day. It was a few weeks before we moved here. I was on my own and I couldn't help listening to them. The son was telling the father about some book he'd read, and the father was asking him what he'd liked most about it. And the son was kind of struggling to answer but he didn't sound worried that he wasn't saying anything all that clever, because it was his dad and he obviously knew he wasn't getting marked on his answer or anything. And that his dad just really wanted to know what his son thought about stuff, you know . . . Well, I reckon that's the type of dad Mr Rutherford would be.'

'Huh?' I just stared at him, wondering what on earth this had to do with what we'd been discussing.

'To Alex, I mean,' he added swiftly, flushing bright red as if he suddenly felt self-conscious.

'Yeah . . . well . . . Alex doesn't *want* to get asked questions about books,' I answered impatiently. 'And he's fed up with how Mr Rutherford keeps trying to get him to do stuff he hates, like making model aeroplanes and playing board games and doing outdoorsy things. And he won't buy a television for Alex to watch here. Alex reckons his dad doesn't like him the way he is and that he disapproves of him because he's too fat.'

'He *is* too fat,' Ben snapped, still looking flustered as he pulled out a saucepan for the pasta, 'and *you're* too skinny . . . but that doesn't mean I disapprove of you,' he added quickly. 'Though I *do* disapprove of the way you eat when you're left on your own.' He tipped some pasta into the pan and sighed. 'Look, I'm sure Alex's dad doesn't disapprove of him either. He's probably just worried about him. Which reminds me . . .' He seemed to suddenly get all bossy with me, which he does intermittently for no apparent reason. 'I thought we agreed that you were going to drink two glasses of milk every day *and* finish all your meals from now on.'

'I don't like milk,' I said defensively. 'Anyway, I saw a TV programme that said cow's milk is really difficult to digest unless you're a cow.'

'There's no way you're allergic to milk, May!' he retorted. I often tried to tell Ben I was allergic to stuff if I didn't want to eat it, and Ben always argued that I couldn't be, since I wasn't getting a rash or going all puffy round the eyes or anything.

'Not allergic,' I pointed out. '*Intolerant*.' Food *intolerances* gave you abdominal bloating according to this TV programme I'd seen, and I didn't see how Ben could prove that I didn't have *that*. 'I reckon I'm intolerant to quite a few things besides milk,' I added.

'Let me guess . . .' Ben sounded really sarcastic now. '. . . brown bread . . . green vegetables . . . all meat apart from chicken nuggets . . . all fish apart from fish fingers . . . oh, and all forms of potato except chips. Right?'

I didn't like him making fun of me so I stomped out of the kitchen in a huff. Ben reckons I'm a fussy eater, but so what if I am? I mean, it's *my* stomach so I don't see why I *shouldn't* be choosy about what I put in it.

That night I had to get up to use the loo – which I blamed on the bedtime glass of milk Ben had forced me to drink – and when I got back to my room I went over to the window to look out. A girl I knew at school, whose mother had also died when she was little (but who wasn't a true orphan because she still had her dad), had told me that she sometimes picked out a particular star late at night and talked to it because that way she felt like she was talking to her mum. So sometimes I checked out the stars too, though I'd never yet felt the urge to talk to any of them.

As I drew back my curtains, I saw a light in the distance that was definitely coming from Thornton Hall. The only part of the main house that was visible from our cottage was the tower room, so the light must be coming from there. But why was there a light in the tower room when nobody was meant to be up there? Unless Mrs Daniels had gone up there again . . . But why would she go up there at this time of night?

My bedside clock told me it was almost one o'clock

in the morning. I stood at the window staring at the light until I began to feel sleepy again. Mrs Daniels did have a secret, I thought, as I climbed back into bed. And sooner or later, with or without Alex's help, I was going to find out what it was.

✳ 10 ✳

That night after I'd fallen back to sleep I had a really strange dream. I dreamt I was in Thornton Hall, in the walk-in cupboard where all the keys were kept, and that I found a secret passageway there. I followed it and it turned into a long flight of steps that led to a big attic room full of dusty old things. There were old-fashioned children's toys and a doll I'd had when I was little, and then it turned out that Louise was there. I asked her why she wasn't in India and she told me that this *was* India. But before I could ask her any more questions, a floorboard underneath me gave way and I remembered that the floor in the tower room was rotten. I screamed as I started to fall.

I thought about my dream some more as I washed up the breakfast dishes after Ben had left for work. I thought about the cupboard in Thornton Hall where all the keys were kept. And suddenly I remembered something else. Alex and I had seen a key labelled 'Attic' when we'd been searching for the key to the garden. What if *that* was the tower-room key? After all, I hadn't seen any other attic rooms in the house.

As soon as I'd finished washing up I left the cottage and raced along the path and up the driveway to the big house, where I rang the front doorbell and waited impatiently to be let in. Mrs Daniels came to the door, dressed in a dark green skirt and black blouse. The blouse had a very high collar with a cameo brooch pinned at the throat. You'd think the brooch pin was sticking *in* her throat from the way she was glowering as she opened the door to me. Maybe she expected me to burst out laughing at her again – only that was the last thing I felt like doing as I found myself standing in the hall alone with her. What if she knew that I had seen the light in the tower room last night? What would she do to stop me from telling anyone about it? Because I was absolutely sure she *would* want to stop me from telling.

Fortunately, Alex came down the stairs at that point and propelled me into the kitchen with him. He had only just got up and he said he was starving, which was clearly true, judging by the huge bowl of cereal he poured out for himself, which was about four times the size of the one I'd just eaten at home. I was dying to tell him my thoughts about the attic key, but I couldn't right then because Mr Rutherford was sitting at the table in the breakfast room off the kitchen, reading the paper as he ate, and I didn't want him to overhear.

As Alex stood in the middle of the kitchen, spooning in large mouthfuls of cereal and chatting to me at the same time, his dad called out to him to come and sit down. 'That's why we've got a dining table, believe it or not – so we can sit down to eat our meals.

I'm sure you sit down to eat in your mother's house, don't you?'

'Yes,' Alex admitted as we went to join him. 'Mum reckons it's bad manners to eat standing up.'

'Exactly,' his father said.

'But she also reckons it's bad manners to read at the table,' Alex added.

Mr Rutherford had a glint in his eye as he put down his newspaper. 'Your mother's right – it's very rude to read at the table. I guess terrible manners must run in this family!'

'On your side, not hers,' Alex quipped.

His father smiled. 'Naturally . . .'

Alex turned to me and added, 'According to Mum, Dad's side of the family has a lot to answer for.' He giggled as he looked at his father again. 'Like receding hairlines, Dad! Chris reckons he's getting one already and Mum says all the men in *her* family have hairlines that are exactly where they should be.'

Mr Rutherford laughed and I instantly saw how much that pleased Alex.

Mrs Daniels came into the room then, holding the post. There was a letter in a cream envelope and a postcard, both of which she handed to Mr Rutherford.

'Is the card from Chris?' Alex asked.

His father nodded, laughing again as he read it. He passed it to us and I saw that instead of writing a proper message on the back, Alex's brother had drawn a miniature plate of spaghetti and a glass of wine. Scrawled beside it were the words *Eating, drinking and painting well!*

'That's really cool!' I blurted out.

Mr Rutherford nodded again, saying, 'It's marvellous, isn't it? I don't know where he gets all that talent from. Nobody else in the family is the least bit artistic. Not even on your mother's side, eh, Alex?'

It was clearly meant in a good-humoured way, but to my surprise Alex tossed the card back on to the table so carelessly that it landed on Mr Rutherford's empty plate, which was full of crumbs and smearings of jam.

'Careful!' Alex's father said lightly, lifting up the card and shaking off the crumbs. 'This might be a very valuable postcard if your brother becomes a famous artist one of these days.'

'Yeah . . . well . . . he might not,' Alex grunted, pushing away his bowl of cereal, even though it was still half full.

'Take your bowl through to the kitchen if you're finished with it,' his father told him.

'Why?' Alex demanded stroppily. 'Mrs Daniels'll do it. That's what she's paid for, isn't it?' He looked challengingly at his dad.

As Mr Rutherford frowned and started to tell Alex not to be so rude, I noticed Mrs Daniels herself standing silently in the archway that led through to the kitchen, listening grimly. And I really wished Alex hadn't said what he'd said because, in my opinion, Mrs Daniels wasn't somebody you wanted to make an enemy of if you could possibly help it.

Fortunately the letter Mr Rutherford had received soon distracted both of them from arguing. It was an invitation from Mr Rutherford's sister, reminding him that it was going to be her seventieth birthday at the beginning of August and requesting his company – and Alex's – at a small lunch party she was planning to have that day.

'*Seventieth* birthday?' I repeated, unable to hide my surprise that Mr Rutherford had a sister who was that old.

'Charlotte is quite a few years older than me,' Alex's father explained. 'She was more like a mother to me than a sister when I was growing up.'

'Dad's mother died when he was five,' Alex put in, starting to eat his cereal again, 'so Aunt Charlotte had to look after him. She didn't get married herself until she was forty and everyone was really surprised because they all thought she was going to be an old maid, didn't they, Dad?'

'I don't know about that!'

'Well, that's what Mum says,' Alex insisted.

'Oh, well, your mother would know, of course.' It was said wryly, but he continued, 'Though it's certainly true that Charlotte gave up a lot of opportunities when she was younger so that she could take care of me.' He looked at me as he added, 'My father never really recovered from losing my mother, so she had to do everything.'

I was staring at Mr Rutherford, thinking that the story I was hearing about how he had grown up was very like *my* story. For a moment he and I held each other's gaze and that's when I realized that he was already well aware of the similarity in our childhoods.

Alex, who was clearly oblivious to the connection I had just made with his dad, picked up the invitation to read it for himself. 'But that's the same weekend as the garden open day,' he pointed out. 'We can't go to Aunt Charlotte's then.'

'Is it?' His father took the invitation from him to read it again. He was looking thoughtful. 'I wonder if Charlotte would like to celebrate her birthday here instead. She could come for the weekend and invite her friends here. We could have a garden party if the weather's good.'

Alex was nodding. 'I reckon she'd think that was cool.'

His father said, 'I'll give her a ring and see. Now . . . are you two going to start work in your garden today? I've got to work on my book, so I'm going to be shut up in my study all day. You'll have to ask Mrs Daniels if you need anything.'

'We're going to have another look for the key first,' I said, before Alex could reply. I was thinking that our search for the garden key would act as a useful cover for our investigation into the mystery of the tower room. 'It might have got left . . .' I paused, glancing in the direction of the kitchen, where I could no longer hear Mrs Daniels moving about. '. . . up in the *attic* rooms or somewhere like that.'

'There aren't any attic rooms here,' Mr Rutherford said. 'The servants must have slept in the back rooms in the old days, I suppose.'

'There's the tower room,' I pointed out. 'Maybe they called that the attic and that's where the servants slept. Maybe we should look in there first. I know the floor's rotten, but we'll be really careful not to tread on the bad bits, won't we, Alex?'

Just then Mrs Daniels entered noiselessly from the kitchen, carrying the same tray she had been holding when she'd emerged so mysteriously from the tower room the day before. 'I've found you a lock for your garden,' she told us briskly as she started to

110

pile the dirty breakfast dishes on to the tray. 'I've asked a locksmith to come here this morning to fix a new one on the door for you.' She looked enquiringly at Mr Rutherford. 'I'm presuming that's all right with you. They seemed so keen to have their secret garden that I didn't like to disappoint them. It won't cost much. I got a very reasonable quote from him.'

'You didn't need to go to all that trouble, Mrs Daniels,' Alex's father replied, sounding surprised. 'Though it was very thoughtful of you.' He looked at Alex and me pointedly. '*Wasn't* it?'

'Yeah . . . thanks, Mrs Daniels,' Alex said, glancing across at me as if he expected me to be the one who was most pleased, since I was the one who had most wanted our garden to be a secret.

'Thanks,' I mumbled, trying to hide the fact that I wasn't really grateful at all. Mrs Daniels had done this for one reason only, I was sure – to stop us from having an excuse to nose around the house.

'Now you can get on with the gardening straight away, can't you?' she said, looking at me in a way that made me feel as if she could read my mind. As the doorbell rang she added, 'That'll probably be the locksmith now. I'll take him down there and show him what needs to be done.'

'We'll come too!' I said, standing up. I wanted to be there when our garden officially became a secret one. Besides, I didn't trust Mrs Daniels not to keep a key for herself if I wasn't there to tell the locksmith that we only wanted one key made.

To my surprise though, Mrs Daniels seemed to relax when she stepped inside the garden. While the locksmith was looking at the door, she led us round the path, nodding approvingly at the piles of dead convolvulus I had created and telling me where the compost heap was where we could dispose of any garden rubbish. She started to tell us what some of the plants were called, which really interested me, though not Alex, who went back to the door after a while to watch the locksmith work.

'These ones are day lilies,' Mrs Daniels told me, pointing to a big clump of the flowers I'd *thought* were lilies when I'd noticed them before. 'My husband planted these. Do you know why they're called that?'

I shook my head.

'Because each flower only lasts for one day.'

'Really?' I gasped. 'That's not very long!'

'No, but because there are so many flowers, all coming out at different times, the plant stays in constant bloom.'

'That's amazing!' I said, staring at the big yellow flowers and thinking how unbelievable it was that they would all be dead and replaced by others by this time tomorrow.

She actually smiled at me then. 'Nature *is* amazing, Mary.'

I watched her bend down to smell one of the roses I had rescued from the bindweed.

'There are lots of different sorts of daisies, aren't there?' I said, as she stood up again. I pointed to some that were growing near the edge of one of the flower beds. 'Are they the ones that Ben says throw seeds everywhere so they can come back again every year?'

'That one is a self-seeder, yes. It's called a corn marigold. Isn't it lovely?' She continued to look around the garden as if she was searching for something in particular. 'There it is!' She pointed to a large yellow daisy-like flower, half hidden by some other plants. The flower was huge compared to the others and it had a big dark button nose. 'That's a coneflower,' she told me. 'My husband always loved those.'

'It's so big!' I exclaimed.

She nodded, carrying on along the path and continuing to scan the flower beds for familiar plants. 'There should be some evening primrose here somewhere. They're self-seeders too. They flower in the evenings. They're a favourite with the moths who like to drink their nectar.'

Mrs Daniels knew a lot about flowers, I thought, as we returned to the gate. I'd have to warn Ben to be very careful if he ever got into a conversation with her about gardening.

As Alex and I sat down on the bench, waiting as Mrs Daniels spoke with the locksmith, Alex started to talk about his dad again. 'Did you see how he went on and on about Christopher's postcard?' he said grumpily. 'Everything Chris does is perfect, as far as he's concerned!'

I wasn't sure how to answer that. I thought Alex was exaggerating, but I didn't want to annoy him by pointing that out. After all, I tended to exaggerate too when I was complaining about Ben – like when I ranted on about how he was force-feeding me with vegetables and glasses of milk because he had an unhealthy obsession with vitamins. I hated it if anyone contradicted me when I was telling them that.

'Christopher's always been his favourite,' Alex went on. 'And it's not like he does anything to deserve it! I mean, he didn't *decide* to become clever and talented out of the kindness of his heart, did he? He was just born that way.'

'He's probably had to work quite hard to get that place at art school, though,' I pointed out.

Alex glared at me. 'How do *you* know?'

I remembered all the lectures I'd had from Ben about how just because you were born with brains didn't mean you didn't have to put in *some* effort in order to benefit from them – which in my case meant doing a bit of work at school instead of just mucking around with my mates. 'Well, he obviously has to practise a lot, doesn't he?' I said. 'There's all those sketches and paintings upstairs – and now he's painting while he's on holiday.' I was only trying to make Alex see that his brother did actually have to do some work and wasn't therefore in such an enviable position as he seemed to think – but my comments seemed to be making him even more irritated. Sensing that he was about to accuse me of taking his brother's side rather than his, I quickly changed the subject. Lowering my voice to a whisper, I told him how I had seen a light on in the tower room the previous night.

'A *light*?' he repeated loudly, which was precisely the reason I hadn't mentioned it until now – Mrs Daniels had been in earshot all morning and Alex had a big mouth.

'Shh!' I hissed. Lowering my voice again, I described exactly what I'd seen last night and I also told him how I thought the key marked 'Attic' might open the door to the tower room. 'Because there aren't any other attic rooms here,' I pointed out. 'Are there?'

That got Alex's attention completely. I could tell

he was suddenly far more curious about the tower room than he had been before. 'Let's go and fetch that key and try it out,' he whispered. 'Come on – while Mrs Daniels is still busy here.'

We tried to slip out of the garden past the two adults who were both still standing at the door talking, but Mrs Daniels stopped us to ask where we were going.

'Just to get some things from the house,' Alex mumbled.

'What things?' She was gazing at us intently now.

'Just stuff for the garden,' Alex said.

As we walked away, we heard Mrs Daniels say to the locksmith, 'I'd better go back to the house too. Come and tell me when you're finished.'

'Quick!' I hissed. 'We'd better run!'

We raced round the path that ran alongside the garden wall, past the outhouses and into the house through the side door.

'Lock the door – then she can't follow us,' I said, panting.

As Alex drew the bolt across the door, I opened the walk-in cupboard and stepped inside, groping about for the light switch. The keys had been hanging on some hooks on the wall to the left of the door the last time we'd been here. As I looked for them in the same place, I let out a gasp.

'What's wrong?' Alex asked, coming to join me.

'All the keys are gone,' I said.

'They can't be!'

'They are! Look!' I pointed to the empty hooks. 'Mrs Daniels must have taken them!'

When we came out of the cupboard, Alex went back to unbolt the outside door, but I stopped him.

'While she's locked out, let's go and check the tower room again. Maybe if we knock loudly enough, whoever's inside will come to the door.'

'*Who*ever?' Alex queried, looking amused.

'There must be somebody up there! Why else would she be taking trays of food up there all the time?'

'Well, we'd better bolt the front door too then!' Alex said, and I could tell that he still didn't really believe me, but was happy to have some fun with this just the same. 'Come on!'

While we were pulling the bolts across on the front door, Mr Rutherford came out of the library into the hallway. 'What are you doing?'

'Nothing,' Alex said quickly.

'Why are you bolting the door?'

'Um . . . well . . . in case . . .' Alex dried up. He wasn't very good at lying to his father, I realized, despite the way he mouthed off about him behind his back.

'In case of burglars,' I put in quickly.

At that moment we heard a loud banging coming from the other end of the house, and Alex and I both knew that Mrs Daniels had reached the side door and was trying to get in.

'What's that?' Mr Rutherford asked.

'It's . . . it's . . .' Alex began lamely.

'*Burglars!*' I gushed. 'Burglars were always breaking into people's houses in the daytime where I used to live! Ben said they were opportune . . . opportune . . .'

'Opportunistic?' Mr Rutherford suggested, looking at me as if he thought I was an even stranger child than he had previously realized.

'That's it! And Ben says you have to make sure you don't provide any opportunities for opportunistic thieves to get into your house, so you have to keep all your doors and windows locked at all times.'

'I think I'd better go and see who's there,' Mr Rutherford said. 'They're making rather a lot of noise for burglars. Stay here both of you,' he added quite sternly.

I nodded, but as soon as he'd gone I whispered, 'Come on,' to Alex and headed straight for the stairs.

'We're going to get into trouble for disobeying Dad,' Alex warned me.

'I don't care,' I replied. 'If Mrs Daniels *is* hiding someone in that tower room, then I want to find out who it is.'

* 11 *

'Anyway, all your dad'll do is yell at us for a bit,' I pointed out, because that was the only thing Ben or Louise ever did whenever I didn't follow one of *their* instructions.

'He might do more than yell,' Alex said warily as he followed me upstairs.

'Really?' I was surprised because I didn't think Mr Rutherford seemed like the type of grown-up who smacked. But then, I suppose I'd never seen him when he was really angry.

But it turned out that wasn't what Alex meant. 'He might take away our garden,' he said.

I stopped in my tracks. 'He wouldn't do that!'

'He might. After all, he can't take away the television as punishment, can he? That's what Mum does whenever she wants to punish me – she takes away the portable in my room.'

'You really think he'd use the *garden* to punish us?' Losing TV viewing time was one thing, but losing gardening time was something else entirely – especially as, thanks to Mrs Daniels, our garden was soon going to be the secret one I'd always dreamed of having. I didn't think I could bear to lose it now.

'Like I said – he might. He knows it's something we'd care about losing, doesn't he?'

I frowned. 'Maybe we'd better wait for him like he said.'

As we hurried back down to the front hall, we heard Mrs Daniels' voice inside the house now. She was too far away to hear properly, but she sounded cross.

'When she gets here, we'll just say that we must have made a mistake about her being a burglar,' I told Alex. 'OK?'

But he was starting to grin.

'Stop it,' I protested. 'We mustn't laugh!' I was starting to feel a bit like grinning myself and I knew I had to keep control of it this time.

Fortunately though, it was only Mr Rutherford who came back to join us a few minutes later. 'Burglars, eh?' he said, raising his eyebrows. 'I think since you two are feeling so jittery this morning, you'd better go up to Alex's room and play quietly for a while.'

'We don't *play*,' Alex pointed out. 'We're not little kids, Dad.'

'Oh, I see – you just act like it sometimes, do you?' Alex's father didn't sound all that cross, but I could tell he was serious about us staying out of trouble for a bit.

'Come on, Alex,' I said quickly. 'We can make a list of everything there is to do in the garden.'

'Good idea,' Mr Rutherford said. As we started up the stairs he called out after us, 'I've got to drive over to the library in town in a little while, to do some research. I won't be back until late this afternoon, so just make sure you behave yourselves while I'm gone!'

119

In Alex's room I sat down on the bed while I waited for him to find some paper for us to use for our list. I spotted the sketch pad I had seen before, lying on his bedside table, so I picked it up. I quickly turned to the sketch after the ones I'd already looked at – and I laughed as soon as I saw it.

'Alex, this is really funny!' I turned the pad round to show him what I was talking about. It was the head and shoulders of Mrs Daniels, looking very like her. A big heart-shaped thought bubble had been drawn above her head and inside the bubble there was a smaller sketch of a man's face – with shaggy eyebrows, fat cheeks and a curly moustache – poking out from in between two giant cabbages. 'Is that meant to be *Geoffrey*?' I asked.

'Yeah. Do you like it?' Alex was looking a bit embarrassed.

I nodded. Before he could stop me, I flicked over to the next page and saw a girl staring out at me. She had a small, thin face with big eyes and a very scowly mouth. I gasped. It was a drawing of me – but Alex's brother had never even met me, so how could he possibly draw me? 'How did your brother . . . ?' I trailed off, not understanding.

'They're *my* sketches, OK?' Alex said abruptly, coming across and snatching the book away from me.

'*Yours?*' I couldn't believe it. 'But they're really *good*!'

'Oh – so that means they can't be mine, does it? Thanks!'

'I didn't mean that! I just meant . . .' I shook my head, still staring at him. 'I mean, you never said you could draw. You just said it was your brother who could, so I just assumed—'

'Everyone just assumes!' Alex snapped before I could finish. 'They just assume that because *he's* so brilliant, that means *I* can't be! And the worst thing is they're probably right.'

'What do you mean? These are really good drawings.'

'Not compared to *his*!' Alex pointed out. 'So what's the point in me even trying? I know people will only compare me with Chris and say I'm not as good as him!'

I was frowning. 'Doesn't *anyone* else know that you draw too?'

He shook his head. 'I hate my art teacher at school. I don't do any work in his class.'

'Why do you hate him?'

'Because he's always going on about how fantastic Chris is. And the first time I ever had him for art, he said the drawing I'd done was quite good and maybe I'd got a little bit of my brother in me.'

'But that sounds like a compliment. I'd have been pleased.'

'Why should I be pleased to have *a little bit* of Chris's talent? He doesn't tell Chris his stuff is *quite good*, does he? He says it's brilliant!'

'*Your* drawings are really good too,' I told him again firmly.

'*Good*, yeah. But not brilliant!' He threw the sketch pad down on the bed as if, as far as he was concerned, if they weren't brilliant, they may as well be worthless.

I could have told him that I thought his drawings *were* just as brilliant as Christopher's but I decided that would be a lie. His sketches weren't as finished-looking somehow as the ones I'd seen that his brother had done. And anyway, why should Alex expect to be as good as his brother already when he was only just starting out?

So instead, I said, 'So what?'

He looked irritated. 'What do you mean – *so what*?'

'I mean, *so what* if your drawings aren't as good as your brother's yet? I mean, there must be loads of famous artists who your brother thinks are better than *him*, but I bet he doesn't let that put *him* off, does he? Anyway, you don't know how good you might get if you keep going, do you?' I was remembering what Ben had said to me about school – *You don't know how well you can do unless you try!* He had said that the last time I'd told him that I didn't see myself getting any A levels anyhow since Louise hadn't – so what was the point in knocking myself out over schoolwork? He had snapped, 'You're not Louise!' before going into his big speech about *trying*.

'But I *can't* really go for it,' Alex said.

'Why not?'

'Because then everyone will see that I'm trying to do the same thing as Chris, and they'll all secretly be thinking that there's no way I can ever be as good as him! And what if . . . what if . . . ?' He swallowed.

'What if they're *right*?' I finished for him.

He nodded. He swallowed again before forcing himself to say, 'What if they are?'

And I suddenly found myself seeing his point after all. I mean, it would be horrible to have everyone thinking you could never be as good as your older brother – and be hell bent on proving them wrong – and then find out that they were actually right and have them all feeling sorry for you.

But what choice did he have?

122

And that's when I had my brilliant idea! 'I know!' I gasped. 'Why don't you practise in the garden? You can paint and draw as much as you like in there and nobody will see! We can take all the art stuff from your brother's room – the easel and the paints and the canvases and everything – and you can paint while I garden. You can keep everything in the shed. We don't need to tell anyone. It'll be our secret!'

Alex looked uncertain. 'But Dad bought those things for Chris. He won't want me messing about with them.'

'Chris isn't here, is he? And I reckon, if you had a proper canvas to fill, you'd do it brilliantly!' I beamed at him. 'Oh, this is going to be so much fun! This is going to be even better than the *real* secret garden!'

We heard a car starting up outside and Alex went to the window to look out. 'Dad's just leaving,' he said. He turned back to look at me. 'Your idea . . .' he began slowly. '. . . it's not bad. I could practise then, without anyone else knowing . . . but do you really think we can just take all Chris's stuff down to the garden without asking?'

'We can't *ask*!' I said. 'Then it wouldn't be a secret!'

'What *is* it with you and secrets?'

I thought I could answer that question for him quite easily. 'Why don't you come to our cottage now and we can watch my video of *The Secret Garden*?' I suggested. 'Then you'll see how much fun secrets can be!'

Alex immediately brightened up. 'Great!'

'But first I want to go and knock on the tower-room door while Mrs Daniels is out of the way,' I added quickly.

'Are you sure that's a good idea?' Alex pulled a

face. 'We're in the house on our own with her, remember. It's not like Dad's here if anything happens.'

I thought about how scary Mrs Daniels could look when she was angry. And I thought about what she'd said the other day, about how nosy children could easily get locked in the cellars here if they weren't careful. But I *really* wanted to know what was inside that tower room.

'We'll just have to be extra careful she doesn't catch us,' I said. 'Come on.'

We left his room and tiptoed along to Mrs Daniels' part of the house, where we found the hoover standing in her corridor. It had a yellow duster draped over the handle and, although there was no sign of the housekeeper, it was clear that she wasn't very far away.

'Maybe you're right,' I whispered nervously. 'Maybe it *would* be safer to do this when your dad's in the house.'

Alex readily nodded his agreement and turned to go. From the way he bounced down the stairs at top speed, I could tell that all he was really interested in right now, in any case, was being reunited with a television set.

'Have you got a TV guide as well?' he asked as I caught up with him in the hall. 'Just in case we get bored with your video.'

'We won't get bored!' I protested. 'It's *The Secret Garden*!' I felt as outraged as if he'd just accused my best friend of not being exciting enough to hang out with. (Funnily enough, even though I'd always had plenty of mates to hang around with at school, I'd never had a real best friend – the sort of friend you tell everything to and who tells you everything in return. I'd always felt like I didn't need one – not while I had Lou, who understood me perfectly.)

'OK, OK,' Alex said impatiently, seeing my face. 'But after we've watched it, maybe we can watch something else too.'

'After we've watched it, we need to start work in *our* garden,' I told him firmly.

'I suppose,' Alex replied, letting out a sigh. He never seemed as enthusiastic about the garden as I was, I thought. But then, he hadn't been introduced to the *real* secret garden yet – the one in my video. And I was sure that once he had, he would feel just as excited about it as I did. Because then he'd see that just by waking up a secret garden, you can wake up lots of things you didn't know you had inside yourself as well.

✳ 12 ✳

I shut the curtains before I put the video on so there wouldn't be any light shining on the television screen and spoiling it. Alex had picked up the video box and was turning it over curiously.

'This looks like a girl's video,' he complained, pointing to the picture on the front of Mary Lennox in her big straw hat.

'It's got boys in it too,' I told him. 'Two boys. Don't worry. You're going to love it!' It never occurred to me that anyone wouldn't love my video of *The Secret Garden* as much as I did. As I leaned back on our sofa and pressed the PLAY button there was a brief pause, then the oboe music started. I was listening, as enchanted as ever, as I watched the opening pictures of the garden coming up on the screen, when Alex started to speak.

'Have you got anything to eat?' he grunted. 'I'm starving.'

'Shh!' I told him, pressing the PAUSE button on the remote. 'Why didn't you say that before it started?'

'It hasn't started. It's just the opening bit.'

I went into the kitchen and fetched our half-finished packet of biscuits for him, deciding it was pointless trying to explain why I loved the opening bit so much. 'Here,' I said, handing him the biscuits and picking up the remote again.

I restarted the tape, but just as I was slipping back into a dreamy sort of mood again with the music, Alex started rustling the biscuit packet noisily.

'Want one?' he asked, shoving the packet under my nose as the big manor house where most of the story takes place flashed into view for the first time.

'No,' I snapped, keeping my eyes fixed on the TV.

The scene moved to India, where Mary was lying in a bed with a mosquito net round it, and you could hear lots of wailing coming from all the people outside who were dying of cholera. That's when Alex started to giggle. The more wailing there was, the more he giggled.

'Shh!' I said, glaring at him.

Mary's ayah came in and Mary shouted at her to go away. And the next thing, she was all alone until two British army officers came and found her and told her that there was nobody left alive except her.

Alex made a noise like he was stifling another laugh as soon as the first officer opened his mouth to speak.

'What?' I hissed at him.

'Nobody speaks like that!' Alex said. 'And the location doesn't even look real!' He picked up the video box and turned it over to look on the back again. After a minute or two, he said, 'This is ancient! It says it was made for TV thirty years ago!'

'It's not ancient!' I snapped. 'Just shut up and stop spoiling it!'

He stayed quiet for a while and I thought he was

finally getting as absorbed in the story as I was, until it got to the bit where Mary first goes outside to explore the gardens. I love that bit in the video because the oboe music starts up again and that's when Mary meets the cranky old gardener and the robin who lives in the secret garden. But as soon as the gardener and Mary began to speak to the robin, Alex let out another laugh. 'They've just shoved in a clip from a nature programme or something and they expect us to believe the robin's actually there in the same shot as those actors!'

I scowled at him. Until now I'd never even thought of Mary and the gardener as only being actors. True, a lot of the time they were in what looked more like a studio set than a real garden, but I was always too caught up in the story to think about that – at least I always had been until now.

When, a few minutes later, Mary asked the gardener what he was called, Alex just about fell off his chair giggling. 'Did you hear that? He's called Ben!'

'He's called Ben *Weatherstaff*!' I shouted, stopping the tape before Alex could ridicule my precious story any further.

Alex just carried on laughing. 'Do you think your brother will be like him when he gets old? You know – grumpy and white-haired and wrinkly and all hunched-up over his wheelbarrow?'

'Don't be stupid!' I snapped.

Alex couldn't stop laughing. 'What's wrong! Can't you see it's funny?'

'It's *not* funny!' I yelled, feeling tears of rage spring up in my eyes. 'It's . . . it's . . .' But I wasn't going to tell him how beautiful and comforting and familiar this video was to me. Or how, when I was watching it, I felt like I was in the company of my best friend. Or how that music made me feel. And I certainly wasn't going to tell him how Mary Lennox was the only person I had ever met who understood how I felt about my mother. (She talks about her own dead mother as 'the Memsahib' because she's never really known her well enough to love her either.)

'Get out!' I yelled at him. 'I'm never letting you watch TV with me ever again!'

Alex stopped laughing, staring at me as if I was a three-year-old having a tantrum. 'But, Mary—'

'GO!' I bawled at him, stamping my foot as hard as I could.

When he had left, pulling a face like he thought I'd gone crazy, I ran into my bedroom and slammed the door. I wished I'd never shown him my video. I felt like I'd betrayed Mary Lennox and her garden by letting him make fun of them like that. And the worst thing was, I felt differently about them myself now. It was as if Alex had taken half of the magic away.

I badly wanted to tell Louise what had happened. I knew she'd understand, because she was the one who had given me my *Secret Garden* tape and she knew how much I loved it. But Louise was in India and my only way of contacting her was by email, which I didn't have access to right now.

When Ben came back to the cottage at lunchtime he immediately asked me what was wrong. I guess he could tell that *something* was, just by looking at my face.

'I had a fight with Alex,' I grunted. 'I brought him

here to watch *The Secret Garden* with me and all he did was make fun of it!'

'How do you mean?'

'He laughed at everything. He said it was ancient and that none of it looked real. He laughed at the robin and he laughed just because the gardener's got the same name as you.' I knew I wasn't explaining this very well but it was the best I could do, since this was Ben and not Louise. Ben wasn't going to fully understand in any case, because he just doesn't get completely caught up in things on TV the way Louise and I do. 'I mean, how can anyone not like *The Secret Garden*?' I finished huffily.

'There's a more modern film version of *The Secret Garden*, isn't there?' Ben said. 'Maybe he'd like that better. I'm sure it would be easy enough to get it on DVD.'

'*That* Mary isn't anything like the real one!' I snapped. 'Lou and I already saw it in the library and we didn't *want* to get it out!' I turned away from him crossly.

'How do you know what the real one's like?' he answered. 'You've never even read the book! All you've ever done is watch that video over and over again.'

'I knew you wouldn't understand!' I hissed. 'I'm going to write to Lou. Is Mr Rutherford back yet?'

'No, and I don't want you pestering him all the time to use his computer. Lou won't have had a chance to answer our last emails yet, in any case.' He started towards the kitchen. 'Now, tell me what you want in your sandwiches. There's cheese or ham and I think we've got some tomatoes.'

'I'm not hungry.'

'You've got to eat something.'

'I've just eaten all of these,' I lied, showing him the empty biscuit packet that Alex had left on the arm of the sofa. 'I'm too full up to eat lunch right now.' And before he could stop me, I dashed out through the front door.

'Where are you going?' he called after me.

'To the garden!' I yelled back.

I was impatient to see it again now that it had its own lock and key. And maybe, inside the garden, I would feel better.

When I got there, the wooden door was closed and there was a shiny new keyhole situated above the old one. I tugged at the handle but it wouldn't budge. 'Hello!' I called out, just in case anyone was inside. But nobody answered me.

The locksmith had obviously left the door locked when he'd finished. There was nothing for it but to go to the house and get the key from Mrs Daniels – or from Alex if she'd given it to him. I didn't see how Alex and I could ever work together in the garden after this though.

The side door of the main house was open so I went in. 'Mrs Daniels?' I called out tentatively.

She wasn't in the laundry room or in the kitchen or anywhere else downstairs. I didn't look in all the rooms, but I called out her name in each of the corridors and there was no reply. Alex didn't seem to be anywhere downstairs either.

I started to walk up the back staircase – the one that I knew came out at the end of Mrs Daniels' corridor. When I got to the top, I stopped and called out her name again, but nobody answered. I couldn't resist creeping along her corridor to try the handle of the door to the tower room again, but just before I got there I heard footsteps descending from above. I darted back and watched from round the corner as the tower-room door opened and Mrs Daniels emerged, balancing a tray with dishes on it. She looked different. Her eyes seemed puffed up and a bit pink, as if she had been crying.

I was shocked. Mrs Daniels always seemed like she was made of stone. Who would make her cry like that?

I immediately changed my mind about asking her for the key. Instead I tiptoed away from her along the landing towards the opposite end of the house. Just as I reached the other staircase, I heard a toilet flush and, moments later, Alex came out of one of the bathrooms.

'What are you doing here?' he asked in astonishment.

I gave him an icy look. Normally I'd have told him straight away about seeing Mrs Daniels coming out of the tower room just now, but I didn't feel like sharing anything with him any more – especially not things that were meant to be secret. 'I need the key to the garden,' I said sharply. 'There wasn't anybody downstairs.'

'Mrs Daniels gave the key to me. Come on, I'll get it for you.' He started towards his bedroom and I followed warily. 'So are we friends again then?' he wanted to know, turning to face me quite cheerfully when we got there.

'Not unless you're sorry,' I replied in a haughty voice. 'And you don't look like you are.'

'Sorry for what?'

'Sorry for spoiling my video.'

'Did I spoil it?' He sounded genuinely surprised.
'You know you did!'

'What, just by laughing a bit?' He looked perplexed. 'You take things way too seriously, Mary.'

We were inside his room now and I noticed that his sketch pad was lying open on his bed. I went over and had a look at his latest drawing while he went to fetch the key from the table. The sketch was of a sunflower. It was good really, but instead of saying that, I just pointed at it and laughed out loud.

'What are you doing?' He darted across the room and snatched the pad away from me.

'I'm just laughing at something *you* really care about!' I answered, grabbing the key of the garden and flouncing out of the room before he could reply.

I was working inside the garden with the door locked when Alex came to find me. He knocked loudly, calling to be let in. I stopped pulling weeds up from the cracks in the path and called back to ask him what he wanted.

'We're meant to be doing the garden together, remember?' he shouted. When I didn't reply, he continued, 'Look, I'm sorry I laughed at your video, Mary, but I didn't know it was so important to you. I mean, it's not like my sketches. It's not as if it's *your* story, is it?'

'It *is* my story,' I said, but so quietly that he couldn't hear. How could I explain that the story of Mary Lennox and her garden had started to belong to me? Or to feel like it did, anyway? And because of that, I was as protective of it as he was of his drawings? Couldn't he see that *I* was an orphan called Mary who was rescuing a lost garden too? And that I wanted Mary Lennox's happy ending for myself? Because by the time she finishes transforming *her* garden, Mary Lennox feels secure and wanted and she knows exactly who she is at last.

'Can you please let me in now?' Alex asked, beginning to sound a bit impatient, and that's when I decided to accept his apology. After all, now that I had started work in the garden, I was beginning to realize what a big task lay ahead of me. I could use Alex's help.

But when I opened the door to let him inside, he was carrying his sketch pad, a handful of pencils and his brother's easel. I'd forgotten I'd suggested that while I worked in the garden, he could practise being an artist.

'Dad's back and I only just managed to get these out of the house without him seeing,' Alex said. 'Is the shed open?'

I nodded as I shut the garden door and locked it behind him.

'I'll have to fetch the canvases and the paints and all the other stuff later,' he added. 'Maybe after it gets dark.'

'You can help me with the garden first,' I told him, watching him put the things in the shed. 'We've only got four weeks. Let's make a list now of everything there is to do.'

'OK,' he agreed.

So we tore a page out of his sketch pad and drew up a list of tasks:

1. MOW LAWN
2. TRIM LAWN EDGES
3. WEED PATH

4. WEED AND TIDY FLOWER BEDS
5. POLISH SUNDIAL
6. PAINT WOODEN BENCHES ??YELLOW

'But we're not going to win the competition,' Alex said. 'Not if all we do is tidy it up. It won't be special enough.'

'You don't know that,' I said. 'The garden will be all untangled and everything will be able to breathe again when we've finished. We're going to free it to be itself – and who knows how special that will be.'

Alex smiled.

'What?' I asked.

'Nothing. It's just that you're really good at saying things sometimes. I bet you'd be really good at making speeches.'

I scowled. 'Stop making fun of me.'

'I'm not. I really like the things you say.' Alex started looking round the garden. 'I wish our garden had sunflowers in it. Aunt Charlotte loves sunflowers. If there was enough time, we could grow some here for her birthday.'

'Well, there isn't time,' I said firmly.

But as I said it I remembered the drawing of the sunflower that I had seen in Alex's sketch pad – and suddenly I knew how we could make our garden really special after all.

❋ 13 ❋

That evening Alex asked his dad if I could stay the night and he said that I could. Ben seemed relieved that I'd made friends with Alex again and gave his permission readily enough too.

The reason for the sleepover was that after dark Alex and I were going to take the paints and brushes and blank canvases down to the garden, where we would lock them up in our shed until Alex was ready to use them.

We had to wait a while for it to get dark and we sat in Alex's room, keeping our voices low, as we discussed the sorts of people Mrs Daniels might be keeping locked in the tower room. Of course, I was heavily influenced by all the films I had ever seen and I still reckoned that the most satisfactory (if not the most probable) explanation involved a mad relative of Mrs Daniels who she was hiding from the rest of the world.

'But don't mad people make a lot of noise?' pointed out Alex, who I knew still didn't really believe there was anyone in the tower room at all. 'We haven't heard any noises at all from up there, have we?'

'She might gag them so they can't shout out,' I said. 'Or she might use tranquillizers.' But I had to admit that my ideas didn't sound all that likely. Not outside the pages of a book – or the scenes of a scary movie – in any case.

'What if it's Geoffrey?' Alex suddenly said. 'What if he's not really dead?' He grinned before adding, 'Or what if he's only *half* dead?' He pulled a contorted face and lifted his arms up to do a really bad ghost impression. 'Oooooooh! I'm Geoffreeey and I'm going to haunt my gardens forever!'

'Shut up!' I snapped. 'There's no such thing as ghosts!' But I couldn't help remembering how Mrs Daniels had told the ladies in the tea room that it was probably her dead husband's ghost who was living in our cottage.

There had been no signs of the cottage being haunted since we'd been there, but ever since I'd seen the light up in the tower room that night I'd had another idea. What if Mrs Daniels had been keeping a *person* in our cottage and letting everyone *think* they were a ghost? It would make sense that now that Ben and I were living there, she'd had to move them to the tower room instead.

I told Alex my idea to see what he thought.

'Well, that would explain why I never noticed her going up to the tower room until you came here,' he said. 'Though I still can't really believe she's keeping somebody prisoner up there.'

'They might not be a prisoner,' I pointed out. 'They might *want* to be there. That would explain why they don't make any noise – because they don't want to be found.'

'I suppose.' Alex still didn't look convinced.

When it finally got dark enough outside, Alex crept across the landing to Christopher's room to get all the painting materials together, while I set off on a sort of reconnaissance mission to check on the exact whereabouts of the other occupants of the house.

Alex was dropping a cloth and some flat-ended paintbrushes of various sizes into a carrier bag when I rejoined him. 'Dad's got Chris a brand-new box of oil paints,' he said. 'Look.' He showed me a shiny wooden box containing what looked like twelve or more silver tubes of paint with different-coloured labels on them. 'Chris would love these. He really likes painting with oils. Normally he has to use acrylic paints because they're cheaper.'

'What's that?' I asked, as Alex put a glass bottle of clear liquid into the bag.

'Turps – it's one of the things you can use to thin the paint and clean the brushes and stuff, if you're using oils. The guy in the art shop must have told Dad about it. Dad doesn't know the first thing about painting . . . Hey, look at this!' He was holding up a proper artist's palette. 'Dad's really gone all out this time.'

'*You* seem to know loads about it,' I said.

'I've learned a bit from listening to Chris.' He put the palette on top of the box of paints and started to look around for a sturdier bag to put them both in so that we could carry everything downstairs at once. 'Did you find out where Dad and Mrs Daniels are?'

I nodded. 'Mrs Daniels is in her bedroom, though the light's still on, and your dad's in his study. No one will see us if we go out the side door.'

The five blank canvases were lighter to carry than

they looked, so Alex took three and I took two down the back stairs. Alex took the heavier carrier bag and I took the other one. But when we reached the side door we found that it had already been shut and bolted for the night.

Alex pulled back the bolt, but the door must have been locked with a key as well because it still didn't open when he tried it.

'Where's the key kept?' I whispered, because it wasn't in the door. I glanced at the walk-in cupboard (where all the other keys had been) as I spoke.

'Mrs Daniels has one and there's another in a jar in the kitchen,' Alex said. 'Wait here and I'll get it.'

'You *have* brought the key to the garden, haven't you?' I asked when he came back, and he patted his pocket to reassure me that he had. Alex and I had argued quite a lot about which one of us should look after the key and in the end we had decided to take it in turns to keep it on a string round our neck. Alex had insisted on having his turn first – though apparently he hadn't got the string part sorted out yet.

It was creepy outside with all the trees and bushes forming dark, unfamiliar shapes around us. Alex had brought a torch with him, which he had given me to hold. The grounds seemed full of noises that I was sure weren't there in the daytime. As a rustling sound came from behind us, I moved closer to Alex in alarm.

'It must be an animal or something,' he said dismissively when he saw how freaked out I was.

'What do you mean – or *something*?' I hissed anxiously, but that just made him grin.

'Stop being such a city slicker,' he said, giving me a playful push. 'There's nothing to be scared of.

You're just not used to the country. You're letting your imagination run away with you!'

We reached the garden safely, and just as we crept inside, the moon came out from behind a cloud and everything took on an eerie glow. It lasted for a few seconds before we were left in darkness again, apart from the torchlight. We hurried over to the shed, which didn't have a lock, but we didn't think that mattered since no one except us could get into our garden now. Only one key had been made – to my surprise Mrs Daniels had been sympathetic about that when I'd explained that I wanted our garden to be as much like the real secret garden as possible.

'Right,' Alex said, after we had placed all the painting stuff safely inside the shed. 'Let's get back.'

We were about to return to the house when I had another idea. 'Let's go round to the front first and see if the light's on in the tower room.'

So we crept round the side of the house and walked over the lawn until we could see the tower-room window. There was no light.

'Are you sure you saw a light from *that* window?' Alex asked.

I nodded. 'That's the only window you can see from our cottage.'

'Look, why don't we just ask Mrs Daniels about it? We can wait until Dad's there, if you like. She can't do anything to us then, can she?'

I shook my head. 'I don't want to.'

'Why? What are you scared of? If she *is* hiding somebody up there, Dad ought to know about it anyway because it's his house.'

I didn't answer, because I wasn't sure *what* I was so scared of. Though if I was being really honest, I had to admit that the most disappointing outcome would be if we forced Mrs Daniels to show us the tower room and there was nothing there at all. But how could there be nothing, when Mrs Daniels went up and down those tower-room stairs every day carrying trays of food?

Alex and I had just gone into the kitchen to make a drink when Mrs Daniels appeared in the doorway in her dressing gown. I did a double take when I saw her because her dressing gown was pink and frilly and it seemed absurd to see her wearing something like that. I briefly thought how ridiculous the terrifying housekeeper in *Rebecca* would have looked in a pink frilly dressing gown, but quickly shook the image from my head in case it made me start laughing again.

'What are you two doing up so late?' she demanded.

'We couldn't sleep,' Alex said quickly. 'We came downstairs to get a drink.'

Mrs Daniels was holding her bunch of keys in her hand. 'I was sure I locked and bolted the side door earlier. You haven't opened it for any reason, have you?'

'No!' Alex and I both replied loudly. We looked at each other. I thought Alex had locked the door when we'd come back inside, but it was clear from the way he was looking at me that he thought *I* had.

'Well, you'd better hurry up and make your drinks and get on up to bed,' she said, placing the keys down on the surface next to the sink as she filled up the kettle to make a hot drink herself. If only we could somehow get those keys away from her. Then we could unlock the door to the tower room and go and see for ourselves just what – or who – was up there. Almost as if she could read my mind, Mrs Daniels picked up the keys and slipped them into her dress-ing-gown pocket before going to the fridge to fetch the milk.

Suddenly I heard myself ask, 'Mrs Daniels, what happened to all the keys in the walk-in cupboard?'

The housekeeper turned round to look at me in surprise. 'Well . . .' She seemed to flounder for a second or two. Then she replied crisply, 'I had a clear-out the other day – there's far too much useless junk in this house.'

'That's funny, because the cupboard didn't *look* very cleared out when we checked inside it,' I said. 'Apart from the keys being gone, I mean.'

'Really?' She narrowed her eyes. 'Well, you know what those sorts of jobs are like, Mary. One makes a start on them and then one gets distracted all too easily by something else.'

She was very good at lying, I thought. You had to give her that. But I wasn't that easy to fool. 'Mrs Daniels,' I continued, trying to sound as casual as possible, 'do you have any relatives?'

'Relatives?' She was looking at me in surprise again. 'What sort of relatives?'

'*Mad* ones!' Alex blurted out before I could stop him.

Of course, that just cracked us both up, despite the fact that Mrs Daniels was fixing us with her cold-est look.

'If you were my children, I'd give you both a good slap!' she told us sharply.

But we were shaking so much with laughter by that time that we only just managed not to spill our

142

drinks as we left the kitchen. It was only as we reached the top of the stairs that I got enough control of myself to tell Alex off. 'This isn't a game, you know! If she really *has* got a relative in the tower room, you'll have made her suspicious now!'

He hiccuped as he tried to stop laughing. 'Suspicious of what? *We* haven't got anything to hide.'

'We don't want her to suspect we're on to her,' I pointed out.

He raised his eyes heavenwards as if he thought I was making too much of this again. 'If you say so. Tell you what! Why don't we take it in turns to keep awake tonight and listen out for suspicious noises?'

I was about to agree to this when I realized that he was only teasing me. 'Well, if either of us *does* happen to hear anything, we should definitely wake the other one up,' I said, frowning.

'I sleep here every night, remember – and I never hear a thing!'

'Well, maybe you're a really heavy sleeper,' I told him sharply. 'Maybe *I'll* hear something.'

And when I went to bed in the guest room next to Alex's, I kept awake for as long as I could, straining my ears to listen out for any strange sounds coming from Mrs Daniels' end of the house. But just like Alex had said – there weren't any.

The next morning Alex and his dad got into a big row over breakfast. Alex was grumbling again about not being able to watch television and his dad was saying that surely having a garden of your own was a lot more fun than having a television.

'But you can't garden all the time,' Alex protested. 'And anyhow, normal people do both. And there are some really good gardening programmes on TV which might actually help us win this competition.'

'If you need gardening advice, I'm sure you can get it from a book,' his father answered.

'I don't want to read a book!' Alex protested, starting to lose his temper. 'I just want to watch a bit of telly in the evenings like everyone else, that's all.'

'A bit, eh? Your mother tells me you'd spend the whole day in front of the television if she let you,' his father replied drily.

'Mum watches telly just as much as I do,' Alex protested. 'She just wants it all to herself – that's why she complains about me watching too much.'

'Can I please go and email my sister now?' I interrupted them, getting up from the table. Before we'd sat down I had asked if I could use the computer this morning and Mr Rutherford had said that I could so long as I ate all my breakfast. (I reckon Ben must have had a word with him about my eating habits.)

I spent the next half-hour emailing Lou while Alex and his dad continued with their argument. Lou *had* already written back to me, so Ben was wrong about that. In her email she sounded just like she was talking to me. She had something to say about all of the things I'd mentioned last time I wrote, so I had no worries that she wasn't still really interested in my life even though she was so far away.

It was almost eleven o'clock when Alex and I finally got to the garden that morning.

'What do you *say* to your big sister when you email her?' Alex asked me as he went to the shed to get out his painting things.

'How do you mean?' I asked, pulling on the gardening gloves Mrs Daniels had found for me.

144

'Well, you seem to email her quite a lot. How do you think up what to say each time?'

'I don't have to think up what to say,' I replied, not really getting his drift. 'I mean, there's loads to tell her – all about our garden and whatever else I've been doing and how I'm feeling and . . . I don't know . . . just the same sort of stuff I'd tell her if she was here, I suppose.'

'It's just that I never know *what* to say to my dad,' Alex said gloomily.

I couldn't help laughing.

'What's funny?' he demanded.

'Nothing! That's not how it looked this morning, that's all!'

He smiled too then. 'I don't have any trouble thinking up what to say to him when I'm mad at him!' He paused, suddenly looking more serious. 'But when we're just meant to be having a normal conversation together – just the two of us – I never know what to say. I always feel like he thinks I'm stupid compared with Chris.'

'Has he *said* he thinks that?' I asked, bending down to tackle my first weed of the day.

'No, but he always seems to be in a bad mood with me, and I reckon that must be because I'm such a big disappointment to him compared with Chris. Chris always has loads of interesting things to say to him – and they hardly ever argue.'

'Maybe your dad gets in a bad mood with you a lot because you're always in a bad mood with him,' I pointed out, thinking about something Lou had said in her email.

'No way!' he protested. 'I get in a bad mood with him because *he's* always in a bad mood with me!'

'Whatever,' I replied, letting out a sigh. 'But Lou says that one of you ought to try being really nice to the other in any case, just as an experiment to see what happens – to sort of break the circle of you being horrible to him and him being horrible to you in return and then you being horrible back and—'

'*I'm* not the one who's horrible first!' he protested.

'I didn't say you were. That's the whole point of a circle – nobody starts it.'

'Your sister sounds even weirder than you,' Alex said, still sounding grumpy. 'What did you tell her about us anyway?'

'Just about you being cross at your dad because he was cross with you for eating your birthday cake so fast . . . and you throwing away the aeroplane wings *because* you were cross – and that making him even crosser with you, which meant you got even crosser with him, which meant—'

'All right, all right, I get it,' Alex interrupted, scowling. 'But I can't believe you wrote and told her all that in an email.'

'I tell Lou everything,' I said matter-of-factly.

'Well, you'd better not have told her about *this*.' He was setting up his easel now, ready to start painting.

In fact, in my email to her this morning I had told her all about his plan to paint in the garden, but I decided it was best not to admit that right now.

Alex had set up his easel in front of some yellow roses and I could see that he was squeezing out some paint on to his palette from one of the tubes. He had the bottle of turps on the ground beside him and he picked it up now, unscrewed the lid and dipped his paintbrush into it.

I stopped pulling up weeds to go over and look as he mixed the paint and the turps together. I could smell the paint mixture now. It was a sharp smell, difficult to describe. I thought it smelt a little bit like polish and a little bit like disinfectant, only that makes it sound horrible, and it wasn't.

The paint Alex had chosen to use first was an intense yellow colour. I picked up the tube and saw that it was called 'Chrome yellow'. He had set aside two other tubes with yellow labels, called 'Cadmium yellow' and 'Yellow ochre'.

'Those colours all look good for painting sun-flowers,' I said.

'I know,' he agreed. 'I think I'll use all of them. I want to try painting something that's actually here in front of me before I start the sunflowers though.' He dipped his brush in the thinned-down paint and started to smile. 'This is so cool,' he said.

I stood watching as he held the tip of his brush a few inches away from the blank canvas and kept it there for ages, as if he was reluctant to put the first stroke of paint on to the surface.

'Go on, then,' I encouraged him eventually. 'What are you waiting for?'

That's when he got cross with me. 'Look, if I'm going to do this, I need you to promise not to look until it's finished,' he said, lowering his brush.

'But—'

'I can't do it if you're watching me! You've either got to promise or I won't do it at all!'

'Don't be so sensitive!' I teased.

'Artists *are* sensitive,' Alex replied.

'I don't see why they should be any more sensitive

than gardeners,' I told him. 'And I don't mind people watching me while *I* work.'

'This is different,' he said.

'Why?' I demanded, starting to get impatient. 'Don't get all snooty about it, Alex. It's not a work of art yet, you know.'

'I'm not being snooty!' he protested. 'I'm *scared* to let you see it before it's done, Mary. Can't you see that? It's just like you with the garden – you don't want anyone else to see *that* until it's finished, do you? That's why you wanted the door locked.'

Of course he did have a point. Except that I wasn't excluding *him* from seeing the garden before it was done, whereas he was clearly excluding *me* from seeing his pictures. Though I suppose I *was* the only person besides him who even *knew* about his secret painting project.

'Well, if I don't look while you're doing it,' I said, 'you've got to promise to let me be the first person to see it when it's finished, OK?'

He nodded earnestly. 'Of course.'

So while he lifted his paintbrush up to the canvas again, I turned my attention to the garden. I had already unravelled most of the convolvulus from the roses, but there was still plenty of it choking the other plants and flowers. And although I had weeded the first section of the garden path, there was still the rest of that to do. Both of these tasks seemed enormous, so before I continued with either of them, I decided to tackle the one thing that would take the least time to complete. I would polish the face of the sundial. After all, this was meant to be a sun garden, so the sundial was a pretty important feature.

I had to go back to the house first, to ask Mrs

Daniels for some polish, but when I got as far as the outhouses I found her in the yard arguing with my brother. She seemed to be the one doing all the shouting while Ben stood there looking sheepish.

'You're not a gardener!' Mrs Daniels was yelling at him. 'You're a murderer!'

'With respect, Mrs Daniels, I think that's going a bit far,' I heard Ben say quietly. 'It's only a plant, after all.'

'Only a *plant*!' Mrs Daniels looked like she might be about to have some sort of fit, she was so red in the face. 'My husband raised that plant from seed! He built that arched trellis for it himself! And every summer since he died, it's grown more and more beautiful!'

Ben swallowed. 'Look, I'm terribly sorry. But it will grow back again.'

'Not this summer!' she snapped. 'Not for a long time! Maybe never, with *you* nurturing it!'

'What's happened?' I asked curiously, going over to join them.

They both turned to look at me.

'What's *happened* is that your brother has just butchered my Geoffrey's best clematis!' Mrs Daniels burst out.

'The really beautiful one that was growing around the arch between the two rose gardens,' Ben added, to give me a better idea of just how bad a situation this was. He turned to Mrs Daniels again, looking contrite. 'Look, I'm really sorry, but it was an accident. I thought those brown bits were dead. I didn't realize the rest of the plant was attached to them.'

'You didn't realize the rest of the plant was attached to them?' Mrs Daniels was staring at Ben as if he'd just

announced that he didn't realize his hair was attached to his head. 'I don't know how you talked your way into this job, young man, but I'll tell you one thing – you're no gardener. My Geoffrey would turn in his grave if he could see what you're doing here. I'm going to see Mr Rutherford right now. As soon as he hears about this, you're going to be looking for a new job. And don't expect any references from us.'

As she stormed off I gasped, 'Ben, what are we going to do?'

My brother looked defeated as he turned to look at me. 'I'm not sure there's anything we *can* do, May. After all, she's right, isn't she? I'm no gardener.'

✳ 14 ✳

Ben and I went back to the cottage to await our fate.

'But where are we going to live if you get the sack?' I asked him, fighting back tears.

'It's OK,' Ben said, doing his best to sound like he was in control of all this. 'The council hasn't had time to put anyone else in our flat yet. We'll be able to move back in straight away. I'm sure we will.'

'But I don't want to move back in!' I said, feeling the tears start to well up in my eyes.

'May, we don't have a choice.' Ben was sounding impatient now. 'Look, I don't want us to lose our new life here any more than you do. If there was some-thing I could do about it, I would. But if Mr Rutherford sacks me, that's it, isn't it?'

'Couldn't you just explain everything to him?' I said. 'Maybe he'll let us stay then.'

'Let us stay? When he realizes I faked a reference in order to get this job and that I've been lying to him from the beginning?'

'Maybe he'll still want to help us.' I told Ben how Mr Rutherford had lost his mother when he was little – just like I had – and how his sister had looked after him – just like Ben looked after me – and how that might make Mr Rutherford feel sorry for us and especially want to help us.

But that was clearly the wrong thing to say to my brother.

'I don't want him to feel sorry for us! He advertised for a gardener, not a charity case. If he doesn't want me as his gardener any more, then that's that. We're just lucky we've still got the flat to go back to.' He went to look for the phone number of our old local authority – or whoever it was he had to phone to make sure that we did still have the flat to go back to. We hadn't had the phone connected here yet and Ben's mobile didn't have a signal until you got further up the hill away from the village, so once he'd found the number, he went out to find a spot where he could make the call.

He hadn't been gone long when there was a knock on the door and I went to answer it, thinking he must have come back for something.

It was Mr Rutherford. 'Hello, Mary.'

'Oh . . . hi . . . umm . . . hi . . .'

'May I come in?' He was looking over my shoulder for Ben.

As I stepped back to let him in I said, 'Ben's out. He's gone to phone somebody.'

He started to look around the cottage and I saw his eyes stop at the history book he had lent Ben. It was lying on the table, bookmarked in the middle. Ben hadn't finished reading it yet and now I guessed Mr Rutherford would want it back.

'Ben didn't mean to kill that cremy . . . clemy . . .' I began.

'Clematis, I believe it was called,' he told me

solemnly. 'One of Mrs Daniels' favourites unfortunately. She's very upset about it.'

'Are you going to sack Ben?' I asked, biting my bottom lip to keep it from trembling.

'I don't know what I'm going to do.' He paused. 'You see, Mrs Daniels seems to think that Ben isn't a proper gardener and I'm afraid she's saying that either Ben has to go or she will. I'm not sure I could manage without her, quite frankly. So I was wondering if Ben would have another word with her. Apologize a bit more. See if that helps. That's what I came to tell him.' He looked at his watch. 'I have to go out now, Mary, so will you pass on that message for me, please? Tell him I'll call in on him again this evening and see if we can sort this out.'

As he started to leave, I saw him glance at our shelf of books. His gaze stopped at the gardening books and I felt slightly faint as I saw him read the titles. I felt even fainter as he began to read them out loud: '*First-time Gardener* . . . *Gardening for Beginners* . . . *The New Gardener's Handbook* . . .' I tried to snatch *Clueless in the Garden* off the shelf before he could spot it, but he was too quick for me. His hand flew up to grab it and I had to stand and watch as he flicked through the first few pages.

'Ben bought all those books for me,' I lied as he put the book back, 'because I'm interested in gardening too.'

'Really?' He turned to look at me. 'Have you read them yet?'

'Umm . . . well . . . no . . . not yet, but—'

'Well, I suggest you look and see if there's anything in any of them about clematis,' he said. 'And if there is, perhaps you'd be good enough to show it to your brother.'

I knew I was the only one who could help Ben now. And I knew that I had to be very careful how I went about it. After all, if I threatened Mrs Daniels she might get angry and if she got angry, who knew what she might be capable of doing? I remembered her comment about the cellars again – about how a child could easily get locked down there if they weren't careful. I decided to write a quick note for my brother, just in case: DEAR BEN, I HAVE GONE UP TO THE HOUSE. IF I DON'T COME BACK SOON, MAKE SURE YOU GET MRS DANIELS TO OPEN UP THE CELLARS. LOVE MAY.

Now I reckoned I was pretty much covered – unlike the stupid heroines you often get in TV programmes and books who just walk into obviously dangerous situations without telling anyone where they're going first. I guess that makes the story more exciting, but it also makes the heroine so dumb that she *deserves* to come to a sticky end, if you ask me.

Mrs Daniels was in the kitchen, chopping up vegetables.

'Excuse me,' I said nervously as I stepped into the room.

She turned to scowl at me. 'What do you want?'

'I want to talk to you about Ben.' I took a big breath before stammering, 'Y-you see, if you'll just tell Mr Rutherford that you don't want Ben s-sacked after all, then I won't . . . I won't tell about the t-tower room.' My face was burning hot and my hands were clammy.

Mrs Daniels looked astounded.

'I've seen you coming down from there,' I continued quickly, 'but I haven't told Mr Rutherford . . . and I won't tell him. I won't tell anyone. Not if you don't . . . if you don't . . .' I lost my voice completely then.

Mrs Daniels couldn't seem to speak herself for several seconds. Her kitchen knife was pointing at me though. 'If I don't *what?*' she finally snapped. 'Tell everyone that your brother isn't really a gardener?'

I felt my insides churning up with fear, but I knew I had to keep calm. 'That's right,' I replied hoarsely. 'If you don't tell on him, then we won't tell on you.'

'*We?*' She fixed me with her most penetrating stare.

'Alex knows about the tower room too.'

'Oh, *does* he?' She narrowed her eyes. 'And does anybody else know about it?'

'No.' I decided it was best not to mention Lou. 'And we don't know who it is you've got up there or anything. We just know you take food to them every day . . .' I trailed off. 'Maybe it's someone you're trying to help . . . ?' I finished weakly.

She kept her eyes narrowed. 'You don't know who I've got up there, eh? Well . . . in that case . . . if you promise to stop spying on me and you forget all about that tower room . . . if you do that, then I'll tell Mr Rutherford that your brother can stay.'

'Oh, thank you!' I gasped.

'But I want him to ask me whenever he doesn't know what to do with any of my Geoffrey's plants in future. You make sure you tell him that from me. I want him to ask me, instead of just going ahead and chopping at everything.'

'OK,' I said quickly. 'I'll tell him.'

As I raced away from the kitchen, I wondered how I was going to explain all this to Ben. Perhaps I should just tell him that I had talked to Mrs Daniels and persuaded her to forgive him. Would he believe she was capable of having a change of heart like that for no obvious reason?

I also thought about the promise I had just made to Mrs Daniels to forget all about the tower room. It was going to be difficult to do that, especially now that Mrs Daniels had more or less confirmed that my suspicions were true. After all, if she didn't have anything to hide, she wouldn't have done that deal with me just now, would she?

I went back to the cottage to tell Ben the good news.

He could hardly believe it. 'She actually said she was willing to give me another chance, just because you told her how sorry I was?'

'That's right. So long as you promise to ask her about anything you're not sure of in the garden from now on.'

'I'll happily ask her about *everything* in the garden, if that's what she wants! I think I'd better go and thank her. Maybe I should go down to the village and buy her some flowers.' I hadn't seen him look so relieved in a long time. He looked a lot younger when he was looking relieved, I thought.

I pulled a face at the thought of Ben buying Mrs Daniels flowers, but he ignored me and set off to the village anyway. They usually had bunches of flowers for sale in a bucket just inside the door of the little foodstore, though fortunately they were never particularly nice ones.

I went back to the walled garden to find Alex. The

door was locked when I got there so I called out to him.

'Where have you been? You've been gone ages!' he said as he let me in. His face was smudged with bright yellow paint and I saw that there was paint all up the paintbrush he was holding and all over his hands. He was going to have to clean himself up before he went back to the house, if he didn't want to be found out.

'Mrs Daniels had a row with Ben and she wanted to get him fired, but it's OK now,' I explained quickly. 'But, Alex, she knows we've been spying on her and she's pretty mad about it. So I promised we'd stop.'

'Did she tell you anything about the tower room?'

'I don't think there's any big secret up there after all,' I answered, avoiding looking at him. 'I think I got that wrong.'

'*Really?* So why has she been going up there then?'

'Just to . . . to check out the floor and stuff and to . . . to keep an eye on it.'

'But why is she taking trays of food up there?'

'Umm . . . well . . . she wasn't really. She must have just happened to be holding them when she went up there those times we saw her, I think.'

Alex looked puzzled. 'Why would she be holding them?'

'I don't know. That's just what she said,' I muttered weakly.

He narrowed his eyes. 'That doesn't sound right to me. Now you're making me think that maybe she *is* up to something fishy. I think we should tell Dad.'

'No, Alex! She'll get really angry if we do that.'

'*I'm* not scared of Mrs Daniels! Anyway, it's not her

tower room – it's Dad's. If he says we can go up there, then we can. I'm going to ask him tonight.'

'*No*, Alex!' I practically shouted.

'Why not?' he demanded.

'Because if you do that, she'll make your dad fire Ben.'

'Dad won't fire Ben just because Mrs Daniels says so,' he said.

'Yes, he will! Or else *she'll* leave instead. And he needs Mrs Daniels to run the house.'

'Well, he needs Ben to run the garden.'

'No, he doesn't . . .' I broke off, flushing. 'You see, Ben isn't really a proper gardener . . . and . . . and Mrs Daniels' husband *was*, so she's been able to tell.'

'I don't understand.' Alex looked even more puzzled now. 'What do you mean, Ben isn't a proper gardener? He must be, or Dad wouldn't have hired him.'

It seemed like I didn't have any choice but to tell Alex everything, if I was going to get him to leave Mrs Daniels alone.

'The thing is,' I began nervously, 'we changed Ben's references a bit to make out he had some gardening experience when he didn't. You see . . .' I looked at Alex, praying that I could trust him with this information – and that he was still going to be on my side once he had it. 'You see . . . he's not really a gardener at all.'

* 15 *

Luckily, instead of being angry with us for deceiving his dad, Alex thought the whole thing was really funny. He pointed out that since his dad didn't know the first thing about gardening, he wouldn't be able to tell whether Ben was a real gardener or not, in any case. However, he did agree that Mrs Daniels was different.

When I told him how Mrs Daniels hadn't denied it when I'd suggested she was hiding someone in the tower room, he looked quite excited. 'So you've blackmailed her into silence, have you?' he said, when I explained the deal I'd just made with her.

'I wouldn't call it blackmail exactly,' I protested, because, put like that, what I'd done didn't sound very nice.

'I would,' Alex said. 'You won't tell on her so long as she doesn't tell on you. That's blackmail.'

'I don't think so,' I argued. 'I think it's a fair deal. After all, why should she be the only one to get what she wants? This way, Ben's secret is safe and so is hers.'

Alex started to grin. 'I'd love to know who it is she's hiding up there. Do you think it's a secret lover?

Hey – that's probably the only way Mrs Daniels can get herself a lover – by keeping him locked up so he can't escape from her!'

'Stop being stupid,' I said crossly. 'Mrs Daniels still loves her husband, even though he's dead. That's why she's so protective of the garden – because it was his and she doesn't like to see people spoiling it.'

'Well, I'd still like to find out who she's got up there,' Alex said. 'We'll just have to make doubly sure she doesn't catch us spying on her from now on – that's all.'

'Alex, we can't spy on her any more,' I protested, horrified. 'We've got to just leave it. She'll be looking out for us now.'

'We'll leave it until things have calmed down a bit,' Alex agreed, 'but there's no way I'm going to forget about that tower room completely!'

We now had just over three weeks to get the garden ready for the competition and I was beginning to realize that three weeks wasn't a long time. The following day Alex finished his first painting and announced that he would help me in the garden for a few days before starting on his next work of art.

I immediately wanted to see his picture now that it was completed.

He sighed. 'OK. Come and tell me what you think.'

I stood back and looked at it. It wasn't what I had expected. Alex had filled the whole canvas with the head of a single yellow rose. I thought it was very striking – especially considering he had never used oils or painted on a canvas before. There was a strange background of grey rectangles and I asked him what that was.

'Those are bricks,' Alex told me. 'That's meant to be the garden wall.'

I looked across at the nearest piece of exposed wall and saw what Alex meant.

'If we hang it on the wall, it should look pretty cool, don't you think?' he said. 'I'll paint the stems straight on to the wall – sort of like a mural. And the heads will be the paintings themselves. I thought we could put the rose over there behind that rose bush – it'll look like a giant rose just behind the real ones – and then we could have a row of giant sun-flowers along the bottom wall where it's totally bare. What do you think?'

'I think it's a brilliant idea!' I gasped.

'Well, it was your idea really,' he reminded me.

'I just said you should do *one* painting of a sunflower to hang on the wall. But this is going to be awesome!'

'Maybe,' he said, letting out a shy grin.

For the next few days, Alex and I worked in the garden whenever we could while the painting of the rose sat drying on its easel in the shed. Oil paint took a long time to dry, Alex had warned me, so I had to be careful not to knock against the painting when I went in and out of the shed with the gardening tools.

Between us we got rid of all the convolvulus from the flower beds and then we started to cut back some of the other plants. Since they had been allowed to get so overgrown and tangled together, I guessed that we would just have to try to separate them again as best we could. Fortunately there were only four main flower beds, each one starting off in a corner of the garden and extending out to meet the path that ran around the periphery of the lawn. The lawn – which had last been cut two or three months ago by Jimmy – took up the largest part of the space inside the walls, and I knew that if we could get that looking tidy then the whole garden would start to take shape.

'Ben says there's a small electric mower as well as that big sit-on thing he uses to do the main lawns,' I told Alex. 'Let's go and ask him if we can borrow it. There's a power point in the shed where we can plug it in.'

'We'll only have to cut the grass again before the competition,' Alex pointed out.

'I know, but if we give it a first cut now, we can keep it under control much more easily,' I said.

Ben fetched the Flymo from one of the outhouses and brought it to the door of the walled garden for us. Then he said he wanted to inspect the power point to check it was safe before he let us use it.

'But you can't come inside our garden,' I said.

My brother looked irritated. 'I won't look at anything, if that's what you're worried about. I'll go straight to the shed.'

'But there's stuff in the shed – secret stuff to do with the garden,' I said, looking at Alex.

'Look, either I get inside that shed or you don't get to mow the lawn – it's as simple as that,' Ben said firmly.

'It's OK, Mary. We'll move the stuff,' Alex said.

'You'll have to hurry up,' Ben said impatiently. 'I haven't got time to muck around here all day.'

Alex and I quickly let ourselves into the garden, leaving Ben waiting outside the door while we rushed to the shed to remove Alex's painting and all the other art things. 'Where are we going to hide them?' I asked.

'Put them round the other side of the shed. He won't be able to see them there.'

Once we'd let him into the garden and inside the shed, Ben crouched down and inspected the power socket, then slotted something into it that looked like some sort of adaptor plug. He told us it was a power-breaker unit, which was a safety device that ensured the electricity would cut out straight away if anything went wrong. He tested the power breaker was working before plugging in the mower. Then he went outside and carried the machine on to the lawn for us. He switched it on and called Alex and me over to show us how to work it.

'I've fixed the blades so they're the right height for cutting long grass,' he told us. 'Later, if you want to go over it again, I can adjust the blades for you to get a closer cut.'

He left us the mower – which luckily turned out to be very light and easy to use – and we spent the rest of the afternoon cutting the grass, bagging it all up and carrying the bags out to the compost heap in the main grounds. We also trimmed round the edges of the lawn and the base of the sundial with the long-handled edging shears Ben had given us. I left the dandelions growing, even though Alex said they were weeds, because they were yellow.

'Gardening is harder work than you think,' Alex said, wiping the sweat off his face with his sleeve when we'd finished.

'But cutting the grass has made a big difference, hasn't it?' I said. I was sweaty too as I stood admiring our newly cut lawn, which was now a neat oval shape with the unobscured path running round it and the sundial sitting in the middle. 'It looks much smarter now.'

'The grass'll grow back really quickly,' Alex pointed out.

'Ben says we should cut it once a week from now on to keep it under control. That's what he's doing with the main lawns.'

'Once a week!'

'We'll have to keep weeding too – everything grows really fast in the summer.'

'OK, but I want to start my next painting tomorrow,' Alex said. 'I was thinking . . . Could I come and have a look at your gardening books to see if there's a sunflower in one of them? It'll be easier if I've got a photograph to work from.'

So we left the garden, shutting everything up carefully in the shed again, and headed for the cottage. Ben wasn't back yet so we had the place to ourselves.

The first thing Alex said when we got there was, 'Can we see what's on the telly first?'

I looked at him sharply, remembering the last time I'd let him watch TV in our house.

'I won't laugh at anything and spoil it for you, I promise.' He looked at his watch. 'It's just that *The Simpsons* should be on round about now.'

'You're *meant* to laugh at *The Simpsons*,' I told him as I switched on the television.

We were flicking through Ben's gardening books, watching TV at the same time, when Ben arrived back. 'Hi, guys. What's happening?' He started to take off his boots.

'We're just getting some ideas for our garden from your books,' I told him. I pushed a glossy picture of a sunflower towards Alex. 'What about that?'

Alex took the book from me. 'That's perfect.'

'It's too late to plant sunflowers this year,' Ben told us, coming to look over Alex's shoulder.

'We know that,' I said quickly. 'We're just looking.'

'Right, well, I'm going for a bath,' Ben said. 'Then I'll make tea.'

'Is it OK if I go up to the house with Alex now to email Lou?' I asked him. 'I won't be long.'

'We're eating in an hour,' Ben told me. 'So make sure you're back. It's spaghetti tonight.'

'OK.' Spaghetti bolognaise was one of my favourite meals and Ben tended to make it quite a lot since he knew I wouldn't put up a fight about clearing my plate.

After Alex had got his dad to set me up on the computer in the library, I opened my in-box and found that Louise had sent me another email. This time she had some important news. They were about to fly to Australia to stay with Greg's aunt and uncle as planned, but instead of just visiting for a short while, they were going to spend the rest of the year there. Apparently Greg's uncle owned a magazine in Sydney and had offered Louise and Greg jobs with him for a year. *I know we were going to spend as much time as possible travelling,* Lou wrote, *but getting these jobs is a fantastic opportunity for both of us. We're staying with Greg's family to start with, so it isn't going to cost us anything. We might rent a flat later if we can afford it.*

In a way I was pleased because now I knew exactly where she was, and we might be able to phone her at Greg's aunt and uncle's house, once we got our phone connected. But on the other hand, she was getting a proper job in Australia – and maybe her own flat. What if she decided to stay there for longer than a year once she'd got settled? Worse still . . . and I felt sick when I thought this . . . what if she decided to stay there permanently?

* 16 *

It rained a lot on and off over the next few days so it was difficult to get much work done in the garden. I told Ben about Louise's job in Australia and when he checked his in-box later it turned out that she had emailed him about it too. He seemed pleased for her. 'Maybe it'll inspire her to try and get a decent job here when she gets back,' he said. He didn't seem to think it was very likely that she would stay in Australia for good.

Ben finished reading the history book he had borrowed and when he returned it Mr Rutherford asked him what he'd thought of it and they ended up having a big discussion about medieval England. Ben was all fired up afterwards and he borrowed two more history books, which he promised to go and discuss with Mr Rutherford too when he'd read them. Mr Rutherford seemed to stop and have little chats with Ben on a daily basis after that, and Ben started talking about him in a way I'd never heard him talk about anybody before: 'Mr Rutherford was telling me such-and-such . . .' and 'Mr Rutherford thinks I should read such-and-such . . .' Normally Ben was quite scathing whenever anyone older than him tried to tell him anything.

I didn't see any more lights in the tower room after dark and it occurred to me that Mrs Daniels might have moved whoever had been there to a different hiding place. I was glad there were no lights because I wouldn't have been able to investigate them now, in any case – not unless I wanted Ben to lose his job. Strangely enough, Ben seemed to be getting on much better with Mrs Daniels now and she was spending a lot of time out in the grounds with him, advising him on the garden. Apparently she'd been really taken aback when Ben had presented her with a bunch of flowers after the clematis incident and had lost no time in telling him that the last person to buy her flowers had been her Geoffrey.

'She's not so bad really,' Ben insisted. 'She just cares an awful lot about the garden, that's all.'

Maybe Mrs Daniels could tell that Ben was genuinely warming to her – or maybe it was the flowers that had softened her – but, in any case, the result was that she seemed to be easing up a lot on Ben.

A whole week passed – and then another. I was emailing Lou every two or three days and there was always an email from her waiting for me, since she had constant access to the Internet now that she was staying with Greg's family. She seemed to be really happy in Australia and she said that Greg's aunt and uncle, who didn't have any children, were treating her like an honorary daughter.

Every day – apart from the days when it rained or when Alex's dad took him out somewhere – Alex and I worked in the garden together. When Alex wasn't there, I went on my own and those were the times I felt most like I had my very own secret garden to care for. It was hard work keeping all the weeds at bay and cutting back everything we could that was overgrown. We couldn't cut back the flowering things too much or we'd have lost all the colour. There were a few non-yellow flowers, which I guessed had self-seeded from further afield over the years, and Alex and I debated whether or not to leave them. Most noticeable were some big white daisies growing in clumps and a plant with pretty blue flowers on it that must have been chucking its seeds about all over the place, judging by the way it was springing up everywhere. Alex said he thought the spots of different colour here and there weakened the overall effect, but I didn't have the heart to pull them out, so in the end we let them stay.

We mowed the lawn again twice. Ben lent us the Flymo each time, so long as we allowed him inside our shed to set the power-breaker switch, which he didn't seem to think we were capable of doing correctly on our own. Alex hardly ever had time to go down to the village to buy sweets now, and because we weren't eating between meals and we were so active in the garden I was starting to feel much hungrier when it was time to eat in the evening, which pleased Ben. I noticed that Ben had a bigger appetite these days too. 'It must be all this working outside that's doing it,' he told me as he made up three cheese rolls for himself to eat at lunchtime, instead of his usual two.

Alex was painting whenever he wasn't gardening. He had taken to wearing an old plastic apron while he was working, because the oil paint seemed to get everywhere, and I told him he ought to get himself a smock like a proper artist.

'How will we hang the paintings up?' I asked one afternoon as I inspected the wall where they were to be displayed.

'I think we'll need special nails to bang into the bricks. We might have to ask your brother about that.'

Alex wouldn't let me see the sunflower paintings until they were all finished – he'd banned me from the shed while each one was drying and stored the ones that were already done with their faces to the wall.

'Your dad's not going to believe it!' I exclaimed, when, three days before we were due to put the garden – and the paintings – on display, I was eventually permitted to admire his work. Like the rose, Alex's sunflowers were huge and bright and quite lifelike. They were a million times better than any painting I could have done myself, but then art wasn't exactly my best subject at school. (And *that* wasn't through lack of trying, since the crowd I hung out with thought that being arty was cool.)

'Not going to believe *what*?' Alex asked me.

'That he's got *two* artists in the family, of course!'

I thought he'd be pleased, but something was clearly troubling Alex.

'What's wrong?' I asked him.

'You know, I don't really think they're good enough,' he said glumly.

'Don't be silly!' Like I said, I thought the paintings were great. OK, so they might not look like they'd been done by a professional artist – but then, Alex couldn't expect to be that good yet, could he? I reminded him of that and he nodded.

'I know, but I'm not sure they're anywhere near as good as Chris's.'

'Chris is older than you – and he's had loads more time to practise,' I pointed out.

'But what if Dad thinks I've wasted Chris's art stuff? He might be really angry with me for using his things without asking. I thought my paintings might be good enough to *stop* him being angry – but I don't think they are.'

I tried to think of something helpful to say. 'Why don't we tell him about the paintings *before* we open up the garden?' I suggested. 'At least, that way it won't come as a shock, will it?'

He nodded, as if that was a good idea. Then he looked at me. 'Can *you* tell him for me, Mary?'

'*Me?*'

'You're much better at explaining things than I am. You can make one of your speeches.'

'My *speeches*?'

'You know – like that one about freeing the garden to be itself again.'

'But, Alex . . .' I broke off, looking around the garden and remembering my own words only too well. When it had been all cluttered up with weeds and long grass, I had imagined that our garden had the potential to be the most beautiful, most mysterious garden in the world. Well, the lawn was neatly trimmed now, the flower beds were tidy and you could see the yellow roses and other flowers that had been hidden before because of all the overgrowth. The path was clear of weeds and overhanging grass. The brass face of the sundial was shinier than it had ever been.

But all in all, the garden hadn't turned out like I'd expected it to. I had to admit that now. It didn't look anything like the secret garden in the story.

The problem was, it was too neat.

'Mr Daniels must have made it like this originally,' I murmured. 'All symmetrical and neat and tidy.' I stood staring at the garden for a long time, thinking that in a way we *had* freed it to be itself again.

'Why is it that when you imagine things, they're always ten times better inside your head than they turn out to be in real life?' Alex suddenly said.

I saw that he wasn't talking about the garden. He was still staring gloomily at his paintings.

'I suppose what we have to remember . . .' I began, struggling to stay positive, 'is that *I've* never gardened before and *you've* never painted like this before.'

'I've never used oils on canvas until now,' Alex agreed.

'Exactly! And we can't expect everything we do to turn out perfectly the very first time we try it, can we?' It was the sort of advice that Lou would have given me if she was here, and for a moment I felt as if she *was* here, reminding me to look on the bright side. 'I think we should start out by telling that to your dad,' I continued. 'Then we'll tell him how you wanted to paint sunflowers for the garden because your Aunt Charlotte loves them and it's too late to grow any real ones in time for her birthday. We'll tell him that this is her birthday present from us and we wanted it to be a surprise, which is why we did it all in secret.'

Alex was looking more hopeful now. 'That's what

I mean about your speeches. You can make bad things sound really good! So when are you going to speak to him?'

'You mean, when are *we* going to speak to him. I'm not going to see him all on my own!'

'OK.' Alex sighed. 'When are *we* going to speak to him?' He looked at his watch. 'We can't do it this afternoon because he's going to collect Aunt Charlotte from the station. She's coming a few days early to help get things ready for her garden party.'

'We still need to paint the benches in here,' I suddenly remembered. 'We'd better do that first. Did you ask Mrs Daniels about the paint?'

Alex nodded, looking relieved at the prospect of not telling his dad anything for a bit longer. 'One of the bedrooms got redecorated a couple of years ago and she says she reckons there was some yellow paint left over from that.'

'Let's go and get it then.'

We left the paintings propped up against the wall while we went back to the house. Mrs Daniels was in the kitchen, and when we told her what we wanted she led us outside. She took out her big bunch of keys, searched among them for the right one, then unlocked one of the outhouse doors. 'Wait here.' She left the bunch of keys hanging in the lock while she went inside.

Alex and I both stared at the keys. I could tell he was thinking the same as me – one of them must be the key to the tower room. For the past two weeks I'd tried not to think about the tower room because of Ben, but it was difficult to forget about it entirely, especially as Alex had reported seeing Mrs Daniels carrying trays of empty dishes down the back stairs on more than one occasion. She *might* have been carrying them down from her own sitting room, but still . . .

Alex bent over to look at the keys more closely. 'Look,' he whispered. Each key had a tiny sticky square label stuck to it. I bent down to see better as Alex silently lifted each key in turn to read the tiny letters. *F.D.* Did that mean front door? *S.D.* That must be the side door. There was *O–1*, *O–2* and *O–3*. *O–4* was the one in the lock at the moment. Did *O* stand for outhouse? There was also a key labelled *T.R.* We stared at each other.

Before we could react further, Mrs Daniels called out to us. 'All right! Come in, but don't touch anything! Is this the colour you want?'

I went into the shed, where Mrs Daniels was shining a torch on the bottom tin of a stack of paint pots. The label showed a lemon-yellow colour. 'That'll do fine,' I said. 'Won't it, Alex?'

But Alex had stayed outside.

'You can help me move the rest of them then.' Mrs Daniels started to remove the pots on top of the one we wanted, handing them to me to put somewhere else. 'This place is such a clutter,' she complained. 'It needs sorting through, but I haven't the time to be doing that as well as everything else. Here.' She handed me the tin of yellow paint. 'You've got a full pot there. You'll be needing brushes too, won't you? You'd better take these two.'

As I carried the paint pot and brushes outside into the yard, I noticed that Alex had moved away from the door. He waved at me to join him, so I walked across to where he was standing while Mrs Daniels locked the outhouse again. He was holding something in his hand and I realized straight away what it was.

'Alex—' I began, nervously, but he shushed me.

'Don't worry,' he whispered. 'In the village there's a shop that makes copies of keys while you wait. We'll get a copy made and put this back on Mrs Daniels' keyring before she notices it's missing.'

'But, Alex, I promised we wouldn't spy on her any more,' I said. 'What if she finds out? What about Ben?'

'Once we've seen inside the tower room, we'll still be able to keep the deal with her about Ben, even if she finds out what we've done. We'll tell her that her secret – whatever it is – will be safe with us so long as Ben's secret is still safe with her. Come on. Let's get to the village before she finds out the key's missing.'

'But, Alex, how are we going to get that key back to her?' I asked.

'We'll say we need more paint. While she's looking in the outhouse, I'll replace her key the same way I took it. It'll be easy!'

I frowned. I had to admit that it did *sound* easy. And I really did want to know what was inside that tower room.

✳ 17 ✳

There was a small hardware shop in the village that cut keys and Alex went inside while I stood on the pavement keeping look-out. The hardware shop was opposite the entrance to the railway station, a few doors along from the village tea room. Alex had spotted his father's car parked in one of the spaces just outside the station entrance and said that his father must have already arrived to meet Aunt Charlotte's train.

'This is pretty lousy timing then, isn't it?' I said. 'What if he sees us?'

But Alex said that if he did, we could just say that we were there to buy something for the garden.

I supposed he was right, but then, while Alex was still inside the shop, his father emerged from the station, carrying a suitcase and leading a tall, grey-haired lady to his car. He spotted me and waved just as Alex came out of the shop.

'The lady says her husband's the one who cuts the keys and he isn't there, but she's expecting him back any minute,' Alex said. 'I left it with her and she says to come back in half an hour. I got these though.' He held up a packet of grey nails. 'They're masonry nails. I asked what sort you needed to bang into a brick wall and she says it's these.'

Alex's father was waving us over to the car so Alex put the nails in his pocket and hurried to greet his aunt. I walked over at a slower pace to join them.

Alex's aunt seemed to know who I was already. 'I'm very pleased to meet you, Mary,' she said, holding out her hand for me to shake. She was elegantly dressed with a friendly face.

'What are you two doing here?' Mr Rutherford asked.

'We're buying something for the garden,' Alex said.

'Really? Do you need some money then?'

'It's OK,' Alex said. 'It isn't anything expensive.'

'Good! Well, do you want a lift back in the car?'

'Oh no,' Alex said quickly. 'We'll walk back a bit later.'

'All the way up that hill? Rather you than me!' Aunt Charlotte said, smiling. 'But that must be why you're looking so healthy, Alex – all this country air and exercise.'

'He's certainly been getting a lot more exercise recently,' Mr Rutherford said approvingly. 'You know, you're in much better shape than you were at the start of the summer, Alex.'

Alex flushed, avoiding his father's gaze as if he felt like he was being criticized, not complimented.

'I think you must have turned a good bit of fat into muscle with all that gardening you've been doing,' his father continued lightly.

'Yeah, well . . .' Alex looked even more uncomfortable, and before anyone could say anything else he had run off across the road. He was heading for the sweet shop.

Mr Rutherford was frowning. 'I don't understand,' he said.

Aunt Charlotte didn't say anything, but she looked thoughtful as her gaze followed Alex.

'I think he just thinks that it's not fair of you to judge him by his appearance,' I told Mr Rutherford politely.

He looked at me in surprise. 'I'm not *judging* him at all, Mary. I'm just concerned about his well-being.'

'I know, but I'm just telling you what Alex thinks, that's all,' I said. 'I'd better go and catch him up.'

I found Alex buying lemon bonbons at the sweet counter. 'You know, you do look slimmer,' I told him, 'especially your face. It's no wonder your dad's noticed.'

'I'm more acceptable to him now, I suppose,' he grunted.

'He says he isn't judging you. He says he just cares about you.'

'Really?' He sounded sceptical and, by the look on his face, he was still planning to eat all his sweets at once, in an act of defiance against his dad, no matter what I said. Deciding that it was my duty as a friend to help him, I took a lemon bonbon out of the paper bag and stuffed it into my mouth.

Alex led us out of the shop and back towards home at a rapid pace. We didn't speak much on our way up the hill towards Thornton Hall because we were too out of breath – sucking lemon bonbons at the same time didn't help much either.

'How do you think your Aunt Charlotte will get on

178

with Mrs Daniels?' I asked as we neared the gates of the house.

'I don't know,' Alex replied. 'But Mrs Daniels is making her a birthday cake – and she seems to be going to quite a lot of trouble.'

'Really?'

'Yeah. Dad asked her to make it. I think he's too scared to risk buying a cake again after what happened the last time!'

'What *nearly* happened, you mean! Thanks to me, it didn't!' I pointed out.

Suddenly Alex stopped walking. 'The key!' he exclaimed. 'I was meant to collect it before the shop closed.' He looked at his watch. 'Come on! We'll have to run!'

But by the time we got back down to the village, it was too late. The village shops all closed on the dot of half past five, and today was no exception.

'What are we going to do?' Alex gasped, holding his side and panting to get his breath back. 'She's bound to want to go up to the tower room tonight, isn't she? What will she do when she finds out her key's missing?'

I frowned, trying to think clearly. 'There's also the other key, remember,' I said. 'The one with the label that said "Attic". She must have taken that one and maybe it fits the tower room door as well.'

'So she'll still be able to get in, you mean?'

'Hopefully. Otherwise . . .' I grimaced. '. . . whoever's in the tower room is going to be pretty hungry tonight.'

Alex knocked on the door of our cottage a little while after Ben had left for work the following morning. It was a quarter to nine. 'Come on. The shop should be open by the time we get there,' he said.

On the way to the village, Alex told me that Mrs Daniels didn't seem to have discovered that her key to the tower room was missing. 'Maybe she hasn't had time to go up there since Aunt Charlotte arrived,' he said.

'Maybe she goes up there less often than we think,' I said thoughtfully. 'Maybe she takes a whole day's food supply up there at once.' I had kept a special look-out last night for any signs of a light up in the tower room – but I hadn't seen one.

'She *must* need to go up there today though,' Alex said.

After we had collected the key – and the copy we'd had made – we went straight back to the house to return it to Mrs Daniels' keyring. But we soon discovered that putting the key back wasn't going to be as easy as we'd hoped.

'Mrs Daniels,' Alex said, finding her in the kitchen where she was busy preparing pastry for some apple pies she was making for Saturday's party. 'We need another tin of that paint you gave us the other day. Do you think you could come and see if there's another one in the outhouse?'

'Can't you see I'm busy?' Mrs Daniels snapped, sprinkling flour on to her rolling pin and barely bothering to look at us. 'Anyway, you can't possibly have used up all the paint I gave you yesterday.'

'No, but we already know it won't be enough,' I said. 'There are two benches in the garden and they'll need two coats of paint each.'

'You go and use up the tin I've already given you and when you bring it back to me empty, that's when

I'll down tools to look out some more,' the house-keeper told us firmly.

So we had no choice but to go to the garden and start work on the benches without having returned the key.

'At least she'll be too busy to want to go up to the tower room herself this morning,' I pointed out.

'I know, but we have to get that key back to her before she does! We're going to have to paint these benches really fast, Mary.'

By lunchtime we had painted one bench each and the tin of paint was almost empty. We paused to admire our work – the yellow benches really did brighten up the garden – then we hurried back to the house, where we found Mrs Daniels hanging out some washing. She nodded her approval when we showed her the near-empty paint can and agreed to have a look for some more paint for us now.

She opened up the same outhouse and, leaving the keys in the lock just like before, she stepped inside. This time she let me follow behind her straight away. 'I saw another pot of that yellow over here somewhere, I think,' she murmured, starting to look for it.

I made as much noise helping her look as I could, giving Alex plenty of cover to replace the key, and finally Mrs Daniels found another tin of the same paint she'd given us the first time.

We went back outside to find Alex looking pleased with himself. He gave me a thumbs-up sign to show that he'd successfully completed his mission.

'What's that supposed to mean?' Mrs Daniels asked sharply, catching sight of his gesture.

'Just a thumbs-up that we've found more paint,' Alex said quickly.

'That Mary and I have found more paint, you mean,' the housekeeper corrected him sharply. 'I notice *you* weren't offering to help look for it.'

'I didn't want to crowd you!' Alex replied, coming forward to take the paint pot out of my hands. 'I'll carry it for you, shall I?' he said, grinning, as he led the way back towards our garden.

'Aren't you having any lunch?' Mrs Daniels called out after us.

'A bit later!' Alex called back. 'Mary and I have got stuff to do first.'

'Thank goodness for that!' I burst out, as soon as we were out of earshot.

'We can take our time investigating the tower room now,' Alex said, still grinning. 'I think we should wait until after Aunt Charlotte's birthday, just in case, don't you? We don't want to upset Mrs Daniels until the garden party's over. Especially since she's the one doing most of the work for it.'

Back in the garden, Alex told me that the next thing he wanted to do was fix the nails in the wall so we could hang the pictures. He got the first painting he'd done – the rose – and carried it over to the wall, where he asked me to hold it up for him. But I wasn't tall enough to get it as high up on the wall as he wanted.

'I think we'll need to borrow a stepladder as well as a hammer from your brother,' he told me. 'Come on. Let's go and have some lunch and then see what we can get off Ben.'

But it turned out that banging masonry nails into a brick wall was a much tougher job than Alex had anticipated. Even when he was standing on the stepladder we'd borrowed and using a big hammer to hit the nails as hard as he could, they kept bouncing off the wall and falling to the ground.

'We'd better ask Ben to help us,' I said.

'But then he'll know what we're doing!'

'Not if he doesn't see the paintings,' I pointed out. 'Why don't you mark the wall where you want the nails to go and then we can just ask him to bang them in? He'll see inside the garden – but he's seen that anyway.'

Ben was busy getting the main gardens ready for the open day and he wasn't too pleased to have his work interrupted by us yet again. But with a bit of coaxing he came and did what we asked. Even he had a job getting the nails into the wall, but eventually he managed it.

'Are you putting hanging baskets up here or something?' he asked us.

'Wait and see,' I told him.

'You know, you two have done a really great job on this garden,' Ben added, looking around. 'It just needs some pruning now, I reckon – but that can wait for a bit.' He smiled at me. 'It's definitely a prize-winning garden as far as *I'm* concerned!'

'Can you fix the blades on the mower like you said?' I asked. 'So we can cut the grass really short for Saturday.'

Ben nodded. 'I'll bring it round for you to use tomorrow.'

When Ben had gone, Alex looked around the garden and said, 'Do you really think it's good enough to win the competition?'

I shrugged. 'Maybe. But Ben's always like this

about any competitions I enter. He thinks whatever I do deserves to win!' I hadn't entered that many competitions in my life, but whenever I did, Ben always thought my entries were better than anybody else's – even though they usually weren't.

Alex was looking at me now. 'I wish my big brother was more like that.'

I shook my head. 'Your big brother's a proper big brother.'

'How do you mean?' Alex asked.

'Well, Ben's not, is he? He's my guardian as well. That's why he gets so involved in everything I do.'

Alex looked thoughtful. 'Do you ever wish he *was* just an ordinary big brother? That you had parents as well, I mean?'

'Sometimes,' I admitted. 'But mostly I just wish I had Lou back as well as Ben. Then we'd be a complete family again.'

'Sometimes I try and imagine how it would be if my mum and dad got back together,' Alex said. 'Then *we'd* be a complete family too.'

'Maybe it's better when you imagine things,' I said slowly. 'Maybe a complete family is much better in your imagination than it is in real life.' Lou had once said something like that to me, I remembered, when I'd been complaining to her about not having a normal family like everybody else.

'When I grow up, I want to have a complete family anyway,' Alex said firmly.

That made me remember what Louise had said just before she left – that she was breaking up our family because she needed to be free to start her *own* family one day. Maybe Louise did want a complete

184

family for herself after all, I thought now, despite what she'd said to me before.

'Don't you?' Alex suddenly asked me.

'Don't I what?' I asked.

'Want a proper family when you grow up?'

'You mean a proper family with a mum and a dad and a boy and a girl and a cat and a dog and a rabbit?' I said jokily.

'Yeah,' he said. 'Well, maybe not the rabbit!'

But I was fed up now with imagining things, especially as my feelings were starting to get tugged at. 'You know something?' I said brightly, looking around the garden. 'This garden isn't exactly how I imagined it would be, but it's still really nice. And in a way, it's better than the one in my video because *that's* just a garden in a story, whereas this one is real. And your paintings are real too and they *are* good enough, Alex. They really are!'

'Do you think?' He still looked uncertain about that as he went to fetch his paintings from the shed.

'Well some people don't try and do anything,' I said, 'but *we've* tried really hard, and look!' I spun around slowly on the spot, taking it all in. 'We've done all this!'

❋ 18 ❋

That evening Ben and I were invited up to the main house for dinner. Mrs Daniels was joining us too and we had been told it was going to be very relaxed, so we didn't have to worry about not having anything smart to wear.

Alex had had to make another trip to the hardware store that afternoon to buy some screw-in hooks and some string to attach to the backs of his canvases. He had completed the task of screwing the hooks into the wood and attaching the string, but he hadn't tried hanging the paintings on the wall yet. He said he wanted to wait until tomorrow – the day before the garden party – to do that. Before he hung them he wanted to paint the green stems on to the walls, and while he was doing that I was going to give the two benches a second coat of yellow paint each.

The garden party was the main topic of conversation at the dinner table to start with. We were eating in the dining room, which felt quite grand. Mr Rutherford sat at one end of the table, with Ben to his left and Aunt Charlotte to his right. I was sitting next to Ben, and Alex was sitting next to Aunt Charlotte. Mrs Daniels was sitting at the other end of the table, between Alex and me, serving the food. Everybody had been served now except Mrs Daniels and Alex, and Ben was giving me a sharp sideways look to warn me not to start eating until everybody else had their food in front of them. I thought that was funny, because normally he tells me to tuck in straight away while my food's still hot and not to just sit staring at it.

'Are there many guests coming to your birthday lunch on Saturday?' Ben asked Alex's aunt politely.

'Ten, I believe,' she replied. 'Six of them are staying the night though, so I'm afraid I've given you rather a lot of work, Mrs Daniels.' She looked at the housekeeper, who was dishing out vegetables on to Alex's dinner plate. 'You must let me help in any way I can.'

'Everything's under control as far as the catering is concerned,' Mrs Daniels responded briskly. 'And Ben and I will have a last look over the gardens tomorrow, won't we, Ben?' She was speaking to Ben as if he was on her side in a way that Aunt Charlotte wasn't, and I suddenly wondered if that was because she regarded both herself and Ben as servants, and therefore in the same camp. I noticed that she wasn't drinking any wine, whereas Ben was. In fact, Ben, now that he was seated at the dinner table, seemed to have forgotten he was a servant and was acting more like an increasingly confident guest.

'What about this competition I keep hearing about?' Aunt Charlotte asked. 'The best small garden, isn't it?' She was looking at Alex and me now.

'Yeah, but I don't know if we'll win the prize,' Alex said quickly, taking his plate of food from Mrs Daniels.

'From what Ben tells me, it sounds like you're in with a good chance,' Mr Rutherford put in.

'Ben wasn't meant to tell anyone about the garden,' I said, scowling at my brother. I was worried that Mr Rutherford and his sister would imagine the garden was so wonderful now that it would be an anticlimax when they saw the real thing.

'All I said was that I'd seen it and it was looking really good!' Ben protested.

'Ben tends to exaggerate about things that I do,' I warned them. 'He always thinks they're better than they really are.'

'It's like how you are with Chris, Dad,' Alex said jokily. 'You always think everything *he* does is perfect, don't you?'

His father looked at him.

'Is Chris your brother?' Ben asked Alex after a second or two of silence.

Alex nodded, shoving a forkful of food into his mouth. 'He's in Italy this summer, painting.'

'Do you miss him, Alex?' Aunt Charlotte wanted to know, and nobody could miss the way she said it – as if it had just occurred to her that maybe Alex didn't.

Alex looked at her for a moment. 'Yes.'

And I knew that he was speaking the truth. I knew that he did miss his brother, even though he didn't miss having to watch how well his brother got on with his dad.

The conversation moved on to history after that. Aunt Charlotte asked Ben if he would have liked to study history at university, if he'd had the chance. How she knew that he *hadn't* had the chance, I wasn't sure. She seemed to know a lot about Ben and me, so maybe Mr Rutherford had been telling her about us.

'It looks like I'm getting the chance to study it further now anyway,' Ben replied. 'Mr Rutherford keeps lending me all his history books and offering me free tutorials afterwards!'

Aunt Charlotte laughed.

After dinner, while everyone was in the living room drinking coffee – or in Alex's case, scoffing all the after-dinner mints – I went to the library to email Lou. As usual, there was a message from her waiting for me and I opened it eagerly. But I wasn't prepared for what I read.

Dear May,

I am writing to ask you something that I want you to think about very carefully. Greg's aunt and uncle know how much I've been missing you and they've said it would be fine if you came and stayed with us for the year that we're here. You could go to school here and everything! Greg and I can pay for your flight and Greg's uncle says he could help find Ben a job here if he wanted to borrow the money for the flight and come too. But even if Ben doesn't want to come to Australia, I really hope that you will. Please think about it and let me know! I'm writing to Ben now to tell him all of this . . .

She signed off in her usual way with loads of love and kisses, but I hardly read the end part of the letter. Lou was inviting me to go and join her in Australia! I couldn't believe it!

Just then Ben came into the room.

'Lou wants us to go to Australia!' I blurted out excitedly.

'Huh?' Ben looked puzzled as he came over and

read my email. Then he sat down and accessed his own in-box to read the message she had sent him. His face was stony as he turned to look at me afterwards, which should have warned me what his response was going to be. 'I can't believe this!'

Then he started ranting. He went on and on about how he'd only moved here and taken this gardening job so that he could provide a better home for me and so that I could go to a better school. He said Louise knew that. He said there was no way he was going to throw all that away just so we could join her in Australia for a year – even if he didn't mind getting into debt in order to pay for the flight! 'And to come back to *what* exactly?' he finished angrily. 'No job! No home! No decent school for you! Back to where we started, in fact. Worse!'

'Ben . . .' I warned him. I had just noticed that Mr Rutherford was standing in the doorway. Goodness knows how much he had heard.

'Charlotte and I are having a brandy,' he told my brother. 'We wondered if you'd like one too.'

'Oh . . . no . . . thanks . . .' Ben replied. 'I think May and I had better be going now.' He fumbled to shut down the computer. 'We've got a busy day tomorrow.'

Mr Rutherford nodded. 'You know, Ben, Mrs Daniels says that she's very pleased with your work in the garden now. I don't suppose she's told you that, has she?'

'No.' Ben swallowed. 'That's good.'

'And I'm very pleased too, of course.'

'Thanks,' Ben mumbled, flushing.

'Let me know if you're worried about anything, won't you?'

Ben muttered something incoherent, looking more uncomfortable than I'd seen him look for a long time. I thought I knew why too. Ben couldn't imagine having somebody like Mr Rutherford to take his worries to. Ben had never had that sort of a person in his life.

On the way home, Ben wouldn't talk about Louise's email. When I tried, he said the subject was closed. He said Lou had been selfish to suggest it and that he was going to tell her that when he wrote back to her. And he made me promise not to tell anyone else about it – especially not Alex. 'I don't want anyone thinking that we might not be here to stay,' he said fiercely. 'Because we *are*.'

But the next day, after we'd mowed the lawn and I was giving the benches their second coat of yellow paint, I couldn't stop thinking about Louise's email and I wondered whether to tell Alex about it, despite what Ben had said. I really wanted to talk it over with somebody, because the more I thought about it, the more I wanted to go to Australia. If Ben wouldn't come too, then we couldn't be a complete family there – but going to Australia wasn't just about being a complete family and it wasn't just about being reunited with Louise either, though that would be great. As far as I was concerned, more than anything else, going to Australia was about having an adventure!

I didn't know much about Australia and I didn't know anyone who had been there, but I did know that going there meant I'd be travelling on a plane for the first time and actually flying to the other side of the world. And I knew it meant getting to see kangaroos and koala bears, and lots more things that were different to the things we had here.

Alex was concentrating very hard on painting his green flower stems on to the wall. He was using a bigger brush than he'd used for the paintings themselves and he'd thinned out the paint quite a lot to make it go further, but he still wasn't getting it done all that quickly. He said it was tricky painting straight on to the brickwork because the surface wasn't flat.

'Will it wash off OK, if your dad doesn't appreciate having his wall painted?' I asked Alex, still unsure whether or not to tell him about Louise's email.

'I should think so – though we might have to buy more turps.'

We continued in silence until both the benches and all the flower stems were finished. Then we sat down on the grass to have a rest. Both of us had paint all over our hands, but we were too tired to care. Miraculously, Alex still had some lemon bonbons left and he held out the paper bag for me to take one. The bag had got green paint on it from Alex's fingers, but fortunately the lemon bonbons inside were still entirely yellow.

'Dad came to talk to me after I went up to bed last night,' Alex said, before I could say anything about Australia.

'Oh?'

'He asked me about what I said at dinner – about Chris. He said he didn't realize *I* thought that *he* thought that everything Chris did was perfect.'

I looked at him. 'So what did you say?'

'I said that since Chris *was* pretty perfect, it was OK with me.'

'But it's not OK with you,' I pointed out.

'That's what Dad said. He said it clearly wasn't OK and that, in any case, nobody was perfect – not Chris, not me, not him, not anyone. He said he loved me just as much as Chris, but that maybe it wasn't always as easy to show me he loved me because I was always arguing with him. So I said *he* was the one who was always arguing with *me* and disapproving of me and stuff. And he said he *didn't* disapprove of me and that if he sometimes seemed to be nagging me about what I did and what I ate and everything, it was only because he wanted the best for me.'

'I *told* you that,' I said, sticking my finger in my mouth to dislodge the chewy sweet from my back molar.

'So I told him that he nagged *all* the time, not just *sometimes*,' Alex continued. 'And he said that was because he cared about me *all* the time, not just *sometimes*. So I said I was fed up with how he always had to have the last word in every argument.'

'You really said that?'

He nodded. 'I said that Chris reckoned it was easier just to *let* him have the last word, but that *I* didn't see why I should!'

'Wow!' I exclaimed, hardly believing that Alex had found the guts to say all this – and wondering too if he wasn't exaggerating what he'd actually said, just a bit.

'Then Dad laughed and said that maybe I was more like him than Chris was and maybe that was why we argued more.' Alex grinned suddenly. 'I'd never thought of that!'

'Neither had I,' I admitted, 'but it makes sense!'

'Come on!' Alex said, jumping to his feet and seeming full of energy all of a sudden. 'Let's get cleaned up. Then we can hang my paintings!'

'They look amazing!' I announced as we stood back to look at his paintings once they were up on the walls. 'They make the whole garden look really cool!' I thought about what my mates from school would think if they could see our garden, and I knew that even they would think it was cool. It was much more than cool though. Suddenly it seemed to have a personality all of its own.

'The paintings do make the garden look different,' Alex agreed. 'It's . . . it's . . .'

'It's *itself*,' I said firmly.

He nodded as if he knew what I meant. 'It's sort of like a trendy outdoor art gallery as well as a garden, isn't it?' he said.

I smiled. 'I think it's time we showed it to your dad,' I told him.

'Now?' Alex looked uncertain.

I nodded. 'Right now, while the sun's still out. Let's give him a private viewing before we invite anybody else.'

As Alex and I went up to the house to find his father, I knew this was going to be the difficult bit – explaining that we'd taken Chris's canvases and oil paints to help decorate the garden. But to my surprise, when it came to it, Alex did most of the talking – he hardly left any of it to me.

'That stuff isn't cheap, you know,' Alex's father said, frowning. He hadn't interrupted while Alex told him everything, but now he was looking very stern and I could see that he was on the brink of losing his temper. 'It's not meant to be played around with. And in any case, you shouldn't just take things that don't belong to you.' It was obvious that he had no idea that his younger son had any talent for art and he was clearly seeing this as nothing more than an irresponsible prank.

'I know we should have asked you, Dad,' Alex said in a nervous voice. 'I'm sorry – but we really wanted it to be a surprise.'

'And we haven't just played around,' I added quickly. 'Why don't you come and see?'

As the three of us walked in silence along the path that led to the walled garden, I remembered the first time I'd walked here, the day after Ben and I had arrived. That was before I'd met Alex properly and before we'd become friends. It was the garden that had introduced us, I thought now. It was the garden that had made us friends.

I unlocked the garden door and went in ahead of Alex and his father to check that everything was still how it had been when we'd left it. There was no reason why it shouldn't be – it was just that now the garden was complete, it seemed to have taken on a slightly magical quality as far as I was concerned. And magic was unpredictable.

But everything was in its place – no painting had fallen off the wall and no bird had accidentally flown against the painted flower stems and smudged them.

'All right, you can come in,' I called out – and Alex brought his father inside.

Mr Rutherford stared. He stared first at the far wall where the four sunflower paintings were facing him. Then he looked at the corner flower bed with its real yellow roses – and the painting of the rose that hung on the wall just above them. He looked over the rest of the garden, taking it all in, but his eyes quickly returned to the paintings.

Alex visibly tensed as his father went over to examine them more closely and I prayed that Mr Rutherford was going to say that he liked them. But before he could say anything at all, Alex started to speak. 'They're not as good as Chris's, I know, but he's older than me and I'm only just starting out. And you don't know how good you might get until you try, do you?'

Mr Rutherford turned to face him then. 'Alex, I think these paintings are brilliant. I had no idea you could paint as well as this.'

The look of happiness on Alex's face right then was better than anything I could have imagined. And that's when I realized that what mattered most to Alex – at least for now – was what his dad thought of his paintings, regardless of whether or not they were masterpieces.

✳ 19 ✳

Aunt Charlotte was delighted with our garden when
we took everyone to see it on Saturday morning. She
loved the paintings of the sunflowers and said that
she would put the one we were giving her as a birthday present on her wall as soon as she got home. Mr
Rutherford was full of compliments about the garden
too and Ben, of course, pronounced it totally perfect.
But unexpectedly, the person who was most delighted
was Mrs Daniels.

'It's just like it was in my Geoffrey's day!' she
exclaimed. 'He always liked to keep a neat garden,
did my Geoffrey.' And she spent a good half an hour
wandering around admiring everything *except* Alex's
paintings, which I got the feeling she didn't really
think belonged there, since her only comment was to
say that she didn't know *what* her Geoffrey would
make of them.

'I expect he'd turn in his grave, wouldn't he?' Ben
quipped, but luckily Mrs Daniels wasn't near enough
to hear.

Mr Rutherford was though, and he gave my
brother the sort of look he generally reserved for Alex
when he was getting a bit above himself.

Aunt Charlotte's guests were due to arrive throughout the morning in time for her big birthday lunch, which was scheduled for two o'clock on the terrace at the back of the house. Ben and Mr Rutherford had already carried two tables outside, which they had placed end to end with a huge white tablecloth covering them, and it was Alex's and my job to take out all the chairs. The gardens were also going to be open to the public all weekend, which meant that people could just walk up the drive and wander round the grounds if they wanted to. Mr Rutherford was a bit worried that people might end up gawping at his guests as they ate, but Mrs Daniels said that from past experience, people generally came in small numbers and tended to stick to the front of the house and the rose gardens. In any case, she had made two signs saying **PRIVATE PARTY**, which she had already propped up at the ends of both paths leading to the terrace.

Our walled garden was open to the public too now, and the judges who were inspecting all the small gardens – including one other walled one in a neighbouring village – were scheduled to look at ours at four o'clock this afternoon.

'I hope it doesn't rain,' Alex said. But it didn't look like it was going to. The sky was blue with only a few white clouds, and it was forecast to remain fine all weekend.

Throughout the morning, Ben and I helped Mrs Daniels as the guests arrived. Ben took any bags upstairs to people's rooms, in between doing last-minute things in the garden, and I helped by serving people tea and biscuits. Mrs Daniels said she felt like she was running a hotel and I could tell that what she really wanted was to be outside, showing people the gardens. She managed to do quite a bit of that in between her housekeeper's duties, which was a relief to Ben because when anybody asked him what a particular plant or flower was called, he rarely had a clue.

Then, just before midday, a taxi pulled up with a guest in it who I recognized.

She came inside and stood in the hallway, letting Mrs Daniels fuss around her. She was being fussed over more than the other guests because she was blind.

It was Miss Johnson.

For a moment I thought that she was here to tell everyone what we had done – that she wasn't a proper guest at all, but had arrived quite deliberately to expose Ben. But then Aunt Charlotte appeared and greeted her as an old friend, and I realized that she was just here as a party guest after all. And seeing Miss Johnson, old and blind and leaning on her stick, brought back what we had done in a horrible, sickening rush. I felt a little bit guilty, but more than that, I felt scared. What if Miss Johnson told everyone the truth about us? What would Mr Rutherford think of Ben? What would he do to him? What would Alex say to me? And it hit me just how much Ben and I had to lose.

Before Mrs Daniels could send me to go and make another cup of tea, I rushed across the hall past everybody, heading outside to find Ben.

'Ben! Ben! Miss Johnson's here!' I screeched, when I found him trimming a bush at the far end of the front garden, as far away from any guests as he could manage to get.

'*What?*'

'Miss Johnson is one of the guests for the birthday lunch! Alex's aunt must know her! Ben, what are we going to do? What if she tells anyone about us?' I started to talk so rapidly that he had to raise his voice to get me to be quiet.

Ben was gradually turning pale as he took in what this meant. 'If she tells anyone I'm not really a gardener, we're done for!' He had let his gardening shears fall to the ground and I could see that his brain was working overtime. 'You're sure she didn't recognize you?'

'She can't have – I didn't say anything!'

'She'll only recognize us if she hears our voices, which means we just have to make sure we don't speak in front of her . . .'

'But, Ben, we're helping out at lunchtime,' I pointed out, because Mrs Daniels had already asked us to help by serving things at the table.

'We'll just have to help without speaking,' Ben said, trying to sound calm, though I could tell that underneath he was as panicky as I was.

For the next two hours it was easy enough to avoid Miss Johnson, who had joined the other guests in a formal tour of the garden led by Mr Rutherford and Aunt Charlotte. I saw her bending down to sniff the roses and I only hoped nobody mentioned Ben's name as they passed the wooden archway between the two rose gardens, where Geoffrey's clematis had come to a sticky end.

At lunchtime, our hopes of slipping into the background were dashed when Ben approached the table carrying a tray of food and was greeted with cries of, 'So you must be Ben – the new gardener!'

'And you must be Mary,' an old lady added, as I arrived with a basket of bread rolls. 'You and Alex have done marvels with the walled garden, my dear. Did it take you a long time to do it all?'

'Not really,' I mumbled, in a gruff sort of voice that I hoped Miss Johnson wouldn't recognize.

Mr Rutherford was seated at one end of the table and Aunt Charlotte was seated at the other. All of the guests – most of whom were old like Aunt Charlotte – were seated in between. Alex was helping to bring out the food too and he was also getting a lot of attention, which at least helped divert it away from Ben and me.

Suddenly Miss Johnson spoke. 'The roses in the walled garden smelt especially fragrant,' she said.

'Yes,' Mr Rutherford replied, smiling at me. 'Mary has done a splendid job of rescuing those.'

'Though I could also smell the paint,' Miss Johnson added, laughing. 'I only wish I could see the paintings.'

'The flower stems aren't dry yet – that's why you can smell it,' Alex said. 'Chris says he really likes the smell of oil and turps together, but I think it stinks a bit – don't you, Mary?'

I kept my mouth tightly closed and just nodded.

'You must have green fingers, Mary,' Miss Johnson said, as if she could sense that I was close by as I worked my way round the table with the rolls. When I didn't say anything, she added, 'Have you found that you enjoy gardening too then, like your brother?' I had reached her place now and, with everybody looking at me, I just froze. Instead of answering her, or asking if she'd like a roll, I sort of lobbed one on to her plate and darted off back towards the house, even though I hadn't finished serving everyone yet.

'*May!*' Ben yelled after me angrily.

I didn't go inside the house. I left the basket of rolls at the side entrance and headed straight for the walled garden. But now that the door of the garden was open so that anybody could get inside, it didn't feel like a secret garden any more.

I felt terrible, even after I'd stepped inside the garden and shut the door. Didn't Ben realize that he'd just blown our cover by yelling at me like that? Miss Johnson had not only heard his voice, she had also heard him call me by my old name! And now that Miss Johnson knew who we were, she was bound to tell Mr Rutherford that Ben wasn't a gardener. Then he would realize that we'd lied on Ben's reference and Miss Johnson would find that out too! What would happen to Ben then? Would he get into trouble? Would they report him to the police? If only I could escape to the *real* secret garden, I thought – and take Ben with me. I was sure that nothing bad could ever happen to us there.

I didn't feel safe inside our garden any more. I quickly left it, cutting back along the narrow path, past the outbuildings and round the front of the house, to avoid the lunch party which was still going on at the back. I couldn't tell if Ben was still outside with them or not. Maybe Miss Johnson hadn't yet told Mr Rutherford about his not being a gardener. Maybe she was waiting until later.

I managed to get back to the cottage without being seen and once I was inside I locked the door, drew all the curtains across and switched on my video. But I didn't feel soothed when the oboe music began. I just carried on feeling like I was about to lose something really precious.

'Oh, Mary,' I murmured, as my old friend appeared on the screen, as sour-faced and skinny and friendless as she always was at the start of the story.

I watched the whole video through to the end. I cried quite a lot, which I never usually did when I watched it.

After it had finished I just lay on the sofa in a sort of trance until there was a loud knock on the door and I heard Alex's voice outside.

'Mary! Are you in there? The judges have been and they've given our garden second place in the competition!'

I dragged myself off the sofa and stumbled to open the door. 'Second place?' I sniffed.

Alex was standing outside in the sunshine, grinning at me. I blinked because it was so bright.

'Why did you run off before? Everyone's been asking about you.'

'It doesn't matter,' I mumbled. 'Did we really get second place?'

'Dad and Ben think we should have come first, and they're going to have a look at the garden that won, because it's just in the next village. They want to know if we want to go with them. They're waiting in the car.'

'You go,' I said. 'I want to stay here.' Miss Johnson couldn't have told anybody about us yet if Alex's dad and Ben were still on friendly terms. She must be waiting until the party was over. But what if I spoke to her first? What if I told her why we'd done what we'd done? Maybe she would be on our side about it. Maybe she wouldn't tell on us after all!

As Alex went off to join his father and Ben, I hurriedly tidied myself up. Even though Miss Johnson wouldn't be able to see what I looked like, I felt that I ought to look smart for her. Then I went up to the main house. A few of the guests were milling around outside and one of them told me that Miss Johnson had gone up to her room to have a lie-down. I didn't see Mrs Daniels at all, which was a relief because I was sure that when I did she would demand to know why I'd run off earlier.

I entered the house through the side door and headed for the smaller staircase. Earlier this afternoon I'd overheard Mrs Daniels saying that she had given Miss Johnson the room closest to her own corridor, so that she would be nearby if the old lady needed anything during the night. Miss Johnson's room must be almost directly below the tower room, I thought, as I knocked on the door and waited until she called out, 'Come in.'

'Miss Johnson?' I said, going over to the bed where she was lying down.

Straight away she smiled and said, 'May? Or is it *Mary* you like to be called now?'

I sat down beside her on the bed. 'Miss Johnson, I'm really sorry I didn't speak to you before. You see . . . you see . . .' And I started to tell her everything.

But before I could finish she interrupted. 'My dear, I've known all along that you and Ben were here.'

'You have?' I exclaimed in surprise.

'I've known all about it from the beginning. Michael phoned me when he received Ben's reference.'

It took me a couple of seconds to realize who Michael was. Then I gasped, 'Mr Rutherford *phoned* you?'

'Of course! He recognized my name and address on the reference. I'm one of his sister's oldest friends and I've known him since he was a little boy. He asked me about Ben, so I told him what I knew. I told him Ben hadn't done any gardening for me, but that I was sure he'd do a good job at whatever he tried. I told him how much I liked you all as a family – you and Ben and Louise – and how I thought you deserved a helping hand. Ben was looking after you in the same way that Charlotte had looked after him and that fact didn't escape him. So he said he would take a chance on you.'

'So he's known the truth about Ben all along?' I could scarcely believe it.

'Oh, yes! He thought about telling Ben he knew right at the start, but I advised him not to. I knew what Ben was like when it came to accepting help from anybody. I said it was best to let him think that he was wanted purely for his gardening skills. Mrs Daniels wasn't happy about having a bogus gardener, of course, so Michael had to promise that if it all went horribly wrong, he would give Ben his marching orders. But he hasn't had to, has he?'

'You mean, Mrs Daniels knows as well?'

She nodded. 'I gather there isn't much that goes on in this house that can be kept secret from *her*.'

'But Mrs Daniels said . . .' I broke off, realizing that, despite not having the hold over us that I'd thought she had, Mrs Daniels *had* still had the power to get Ben sacked. So in a way she hadn't tricked me completely, when she'd made that deal with me about Ben.

Just then we heard a noise above our heads.

Miss Johnson sighed. 'I must say that whoever's in that room above me has been making quite a racket since I came up here to have a rest.'

I stared up at the ceiling. 'What sort of racket?' I asked, trying to keep my voice steady.

'Oh, just footsteps . . . a chair scraping . . . voices . . .'

'*Voices?*'

'Arguing, I think.'

'Do you know where Mrs Daniels is?' I asked her.

'She said she was going up to her room for a lie-down too. She said she had a headache and that she'd clear up the lunch things a bit later on when she was feeling better.'

I didn't believe that. I knew where Mrs Daniels was – and I knew that she wasn't in her room. Briefly I considered confronting the housekeeper when she came down from the tower room, but then Miss Johnson said, 'Let's go back downstairs and you can take me for another stroll in that lovely walled garden of yours.' She was holding out her hand for me to help her up.

Mrs Daniels – and whoever she had in the tower room – would have to wait, I decided. Anyway, it would be much better to confront her when Alex was with me.

'Is Mr Rutherford going to tell Ben that he knows the truth now?' I asked Miss Johnson as I led her carefully down the stairs.

'Oh, yes. I think he's planning to tell him later today. He's got something else he wants to propose to him as well, I believe.'

'What's that?' I asked warily.

'Oh, I don't think it's for me to say. Don't worry! You'll find out soon enough.'

As we reached the bottom of the stairs, we heard footsteps behind us and I turned to see Mrs Daniels following us. As usual she was carrying a tray.

'Are you feeling better, Mrs Daniels?' I asked, not bothering to keep the sarcasm out of my voice. 'Has your *headache* gone yet?'

'Just about,' the housekeeper replied crisply. 'And how are *you* feeling after your little episode at lunchtime? Have your *manners* come back yet?'

I scowled at her and thought how satisfying it would be to bang her over the head with that tray.

Mr Rutherford had his talk with Ben that afternoon after they got back from inspecting the garden that had won first prize in the competition. Ben told me afterwards that Mr Rutherford had been quite matter-of-fact about knowing that he wasn't really a gardener and had been quick to make it clear that he had no intention of sacking Ben.

Ben had been shocked at first to find out that his employer had known about him from the beginning – and then hugely relieved as he realized that he didn't have to pretend any longer and that his job at Thornton Hall was safe. And then, of course, Ben had wanted to know *why* Mr Rutherford had employed him in the first place. That bit had been the most difficult for Ben to swallow, by the sound of it. Mr Rutherford had told him straight out that he and Miss Johnson had both thought we could do with a bit of help. Just as Miss Johnson had predicted, Ben hadn't liked that one bit and had launched into his usual rant about how he wasn't a charity case.

But Mr Rutherford had got impatient with him then and told him that part of being grown up was realizing that accepting help from another person was sometimes a necessary thing to do.

Ben flushed as he recounted what had happened next. 'I sort of lost it then! I mean, how dare he lecture me on what being a grown-up was all about, you know? So I said he could stop being so patronizing, because I'd grown up a long time ago, thanks very much – without any help from *him* or anybody else!'

'Wow!' I gasped. 'You really said that?'

'Yeah . . . unfortunately. So he said that maybe that was my problem and then he really laid into me for speaking to him like that. I felt like I was back at school getting into trouble from the head or something.'

'Alex *said* his dad always has to have the last word in every argument,' I said sympathetically.

'Yeah, well, this wasn't just *one* word – it was a whole earful of them. I guess I shouldn't have spoken to him like that though,' he added gloomily. 'I mean, he is my boss, after all, and he *has* been pretty good to us. I did apologize afterwards, but he said he was going to come round to see me tomorrow night to talk to me some more. I just hope he doesn't change his mind about keeping me on here.'

'We can always go to Australia if he does,' I said lightly (which *so* wasn't the right thing to say at that point, but I just couldn't help it).

On Sunday evening, when Mr Rutherford came to the cottage, Ben was nothing but respectful, and I could see how relieved he was when Mr Rutherford confirmed that he was still happy to let Ben stay on as gardener for as long as he wanted. But then he added that he couldn't help wondering whether that was the best thing for Ben.

'What do you mean?' Ben said hoarsely, and I felt my insides go tense as I waited to hear what was coming next. I'd thought that our life here was secure now that everybody knew the truth. But maybe it wasn't.

'I've been making some enquiries on your behalf, Ben. You got such good A-level results and you were offered a place at university to study history before. I really don't see why you shouldn't apply for a university place now as an older student. I'd be more than willing to act as your referee.'

Ben looked flabbergasted. 'But I can't just go off to university! You know that!' He looked at me as he said it.

'Mary could come and live with us during term-time if you wanted,' Mr Rutherford said. 'Goodness knows there's enough room! You could come back and work as our gardener during the holidays – and I can get some other help when you're not here. Mrs Daniels is keen to do more in the garden herself, so I might hire someone else to help out in the house. Anyway, Mrs Daniels and I would gladly take care of Mary while you were away.'

Ben was staring at him speechlessly. 'I don't have any money,' he finally croaked.

'You'd have to get a student loan, which you could pay back once you started earning. And you're a hard worker, so I know you'll find part-time work to help bring in some funds while you're studying. But the other thing is this: my aunt who left me this house also left me a sizeable sum of money to go with it. She loved her gardens and I'm sure she'd be very pleased if, in return for your continuing to work here in the holidays, we sorted you out with some sort of sponsorship to help you with the fees.'

'I couldn't accept any money from you!' Ben said hotly.

'It's not charity, Ben, believe me! It's a way of keeping you here as our gardener, at least until you finish university. You've no idea how hard it's been to find someone to be the gardener here who Mrs Daniels *doesn't* feel is making her Geoffrey turn in his grave!'

To my amazement Ben actually smiled at that. It was the first time I'd ever seen him smile when somebody offered him financial help.

'I don't know . . .' he murmured, but usually he *did* know – that was the thing.

'I don't want to stay at Thornton Hall on my own,' I said quickly, just to remind everyone that it was *my* future we were talking about here, not just Ben's.

'You wouldn't be on your own, Mary,' Mr Rutherford said. 'Mrs Daniels or I would always be here. And Ben would be spending a lot of time here too. University terms are much shorter than school ones, you know. Alex will go back to live with his mother, of course, but I'm sure he'll come to visit at the weekends sometimes – and he'll certainly be back in the school holidays. Ben may well come back for some weekends too, if he doesn't apply to a university too far away.'

I shook my head. It wasn't just that I didn't like the idea of staying at Thornton Hall – which I didn't, chiefly because of Mrs Daniels and the weird goings-on up in the tower room. The thing was, I had a much better idea.

'I'd rather go to Australia to stay with Louise,' I said.

'Come off it, May—' Ben began crossly, but I interrupted him.

'Why can't I go, when it's what I really want to do?' I said.

'You know why!'

'No, I don't! Look, you really want to go to university, don't you?' I challenged him. 'So why don't we both just do what we really *want* for a change?'

Ben stared at me. He opened his mouth to speak, then closed it again.

'What's all this about Australia?' Mr Rutherford wanted to know.

And slowly, looking as if his whole world had just been turned upside down, Ben began to explain.

✳ 20 ✳

Ben emailed Louise the following lunchtime and asked for her phone number at Greg's aunt and uncle's house so he could talk to her directly about what she'd suggested. He then spent most of the afternoon on the Internet in the library at Thornton Hall, researching what history courses were available, how he could apply for them and how much they were going to cost. He kept telling me that he hadn't yet decided anything for definite and that he would let me know when he had.

Now that Mrs Daniels no longer had any hold over us – and since we had our own key to the tower room – Alex and I both knew we could go up there whenever we wanted. So why we decided to schedule our expedition to the top of the house for midnight on Monday, I wasn't entirely sure.

'We have to drop in on them when they least expect it,' Alex argued on Monday afternoon, when I suggested that a trip to the tower room in daylight might be a better idea. 'It'll be much safer that way.'

'Safer?' I queried.

'Safer for *us*. After all, we don't know who or *what* might be up there, do we? It'll be much better to get a look at them while they're sleeping.' Alex sounded to me like he was getting a bit of a kick out of trying to freak me out.

'I wouldn't worry too much,' I said coolly. 'It's probably just a relative – and not even a mad one. We'd know if they didn't want to be there. They'd be banging on the door to get out.'

'Yeah, but how do you know it's a *person*?'

'Don't tell me it's a ghost again, because you know I don't believe in them!' I snapped.

He grinned. 'Well, *I* reckon it could be an animal!'

'An *animal*?'

'I reckon Mrs Daniels might be keeping a pet up there. Those trays of food could be for it – not for a person at all.'

'She wouldn't serve food to an animal on a china plate, would she?' I protested. 'Or take it tea in a pot!'

'Maybe she just puts those things on the tray to hide what she's *really* taking up there. Maybe she's got some kind of pet food hidden in that teapot.'

'But we'd *hear* an animal,' I said dismissively. 'It would make some sort of noise.'

'What if it's something that doesn't make a lot of noise – like a rabbit or a rat or a tortoise?'

'Well, what about the voices Miss Johnson heard? She actually heard Mrs Daniels arguing with someone.'

'Maybe what she heard was Mrs Daniels talking out loud to her pet. My mum talks to our cat all the time. She argues with it too! She says stuff like, *I told you not to throw up on that carpet! If you're going to throw up, why can't you do it outside?* I mean, that might sound like a conversation if you weren't close enough to hear properly.'

I pulled a face because I still thought his idea was pretty far-fetched. 'Why would Mrs Daniels want to keep her pet a secret?' I challenged him.

'I don't know. Maybe she thinks Dad wouldn't let her keep it in the house if she told him. Maybe it's something really weird – like a snake!'

Now, *that* I could believe! A snake was just the sort of pet I could imagine Mrs Daniels having.

'Maybe she takes it a whole teapot full of live mice every day,' Alex went on. 'And then she *hand-feeds* them to it.'

'Don't be revolting!' I said sharply – but I couldn't help remembering how I'd caught Mrs Daniels looking for mice under the sofa that day in our cottage.

'Look, whatever's going on,' Alex said, 'I think it's time we found out. So I've asked Dad if you can sleep over tonight and he says you can.'

That evening Alex and I played Monopoly with his dad and also with Ben, who had come up to the house to ask Mr Rutherford's advice about university courses and ended up staying for supper. Aunt Charlotte had gone home that morning, taking one of Alex's sunflower paintings with her. Mr Rutherford said he wanted to hang one of the sunflowers next to Chris's paintings on the upstairs landing, and Alex was going to take the other two sunflower pictures home with him. The painting of the rose he had given to me.

'Yellow roses will always make me think of you,' he told me, grinning. 'Yellow roses and convolvulus!'

Alex and I went to bed at half-past ten, waiting in our bedrooms for the rest of the house to follow suit.

We heard Mr Rutherford come up to bed about half an hour later, though we knew he'd be awake for a while, reading. Mrs Daniels had gone upstairs for the night much earlier on, but we weren't sure whether or not she had gone to bed.

Alex knocked on my door at one minute to midnight and when I opened it, he was shining a torch on his face, pretending to be some sort of ghoul.

'I'm not coming with you if you're just going to muck about!' I whispered crossly.

He grinned and shone the light ahead of us along the landing. 'Don't be such a wimp! Dad's definitely asleep, because I just stood outside his door and heard him snoring. So come on!' He led the way along the landing to Mrs Daniels' corridor, then stopped. 'I wonder if *she's* still awake.'

We turned off the torch and crept past her bathroom and bedroom. There were no lights visible under any of her doors. 'Have you got the key?' I whispered to Alex when we came to the door that led up to the tower.

He nodded, switching the torch back on and shining it on to the lock. He quickly slipped in the key and turned it. The door creaked slightly as he opened it and we both froze, but the house remained silent. Alex shone the light on the staircase ahead of us. It was a spiral one that seemed to twist upwards at a very steep angle.

'Do you want to go first?' he whispered.

'Why? Don't you?' I hissed back.

'I bet you're too scared to go first, aren't you?' he teased. 'Girls always are!'

'I am not!' I grabbed the torch from him and stepped on to the first stair. I could feel my heart

215

beating now. What if Mrs Daniels woke up and caught us? What if she shut the door behind us and locked us in the tower room forever?

But I knew those thoughts were silly. Mrs Daniels wasn't *that* evil and, in any case, Alex's dad was here in the house with us. If we suddenly disappeared then he would come looking for us.

As I climbed the steps I thought I heard a muffled sob coming from above. 'I think someone's crying up there,' I whispered, turning round to tell Alex.

'I can't hear anything,' he whispered back.

The staircase was shorter than I'd imagined it would be. We soon reached a closed door at the top of it and heard the sound of someone blowing their nose.

'Shall we go in?' I asked Alex, who, since he had heard the nose-blowing, was looking a lot less relaxed.

Then we heard crying again.

Suddenly, whatever was inside that tower room didn't seem so scary. 'They might need our help,' I hissed, and I knocked on the door.

There was no response.

I knocked again. Still the muffled sobs continued.

'I'm going in,' I said. 'You keep a look-out for Mrs Daniels.'

The door wasn't locked and it pushed open easily. The only light inside came from a portable television set on the opposite side of the room. It seemed to be showing an old black-and-white movie. There was no sound coming from the set, but an armchair was pulled up close to it and somebody was sitting there with their back to me.

I stepped closer and called out, 'Hello?' My mouth felt completely dry.

There was no reply. I shone the torch on to the person in the chair and stepped further into the room at the same time. As the figure stood up, I felt the floor give way beneath my foot. As I stumbled forwards, losing my balance, I saw that I was face to face with Mrs Daniels herself. She had headphones on which were plugged into the television.

'Mary!' she cried out, pulling off the earphones. 'Mind the floor!'

But it was too late. My right foot had already gone through the floor and my left foot – and the rest of me – seemed about to follow. The torch fell from my hand and I screamed as I felt myself falling.

Mrs Daniels switched on the light and told me not to panic, which was difficult as there was dust everywhere and it was going in my eyes so that I couldn't see properly. I started to cough and all I wanted was to feel firm ground beneath my feet again. She barked at Alex to stay in the doorway as she started to pick her way around the safe bits of the floor towards me. 'I told you this floor was dangerous,' she grunted. 'That's why you weren't meant to come up here.'

'But *you* came up here,' I argued, as I clung on to a beam of wood with both arms, trying to get my legs back up from the hole I had just made in the floor and through which the entire lower half of my body had now disappeared.

'I'm an adult. I'm allowed to take stupid risks with my own life,' Mrs Daniels said sharply. 'Alex, we're going to need help here. I think you'd better go and fetch your father.'

'He won't like it if he sees that,' Alex warned her, pointing at the silent television in an awed sort of a way, like it was some sort of apparition.

'He'll like it even less if Mary falls through the floor to her death,' the housekeeper snapped. 'Now hurry up!'

'I'm not really going to fall that far, am I?' I asked, making the mistake of looking beneath me. It was a long way down into the darkened room below.

'We both will if this floor caves in any more,' Mrs Daniels said. 'Now just keep still and you'll be fine.'

'I don't understand,' I said as we waited for Alex to bring help. 'Why are you up here on your own? And why were you crying?'

'I was watching a very weepy film. Don't you cry when you watch weepy films? Now stop talking and concentrate on keeping still, please!'

It wasn't long before Alex arrived with his father. Once Mr Rutherford – looking very sleepy and dishevelled in his dressing-gown – had pulled me to safety and seen us all back down to the main landing, he went to inspect the damage I had done to the bedroom below – the one where Miss Johnson had been sleeping.

'Miss Johnson *said* she could hear voices!' I exclaimed.

Mrs Daniels grunted that she didn't always put her headphones on to watch her television set. Sometimes, especially during the daytime, she sat and watched with the volume turned down low. But clearly not low enough for Miss Johnson's bat-like ears, she added tartly.

We all went downstairs to the kitchen, where Mrs Daniels promptly put on the kettle to make us all a cup of tea and Alex headed straight for the chocolate biscuits. For once Mr Rutherford didn't stop him. He wanted an explanation about what had just happened and, before Alex or I could speak, Mrs Daniels started to.

'I was afraid I might lose my job when you first arrived here,' she told her employer, 'so I'm sorry to say I tried to ingratiate myself with you in any way I could. I told you I didn't approve of television any more than you did when you mentioned how you felt about it. At that time I still had the old portable down in the cottage, which I knew I could go and watch whenever I wanted – until Ben and Mary arrived, of course. That's when I thought of moving the television up here. Most of the tower-room floor is safe enough – apart from that rotten part in the middle. I accidentally left the remote control behind though,' she said, looking at me. 'That's what I was looking for the day I showed you and Ben the cottage. I thought it might have got kicked underneath the sofa. In the end I found it behind the cushion on the armchair.'

'So all those times we saw you carrying a tray,' Alex said, unable to keep the amazement out of his voice, 'that was just for you?'

'Of course!' She sounded impatient. 'Haven't you ever heard of people having TV dinners?' She told us that she liked to eat her evening meal and her lunch in front of either the news or an episode of her favourite soap, although if there happened to be an old weepy movie on at either of those times, she'd plump for that instead.

'Mrs Daniels, I had no idea . . .' Mr Rutherford began, sounding like he was talking about some sort of illness or disability that he hadn't known she had until now.

And that's when Mrs Daniels suddenly lost her temper. 'I haven't got a disease!' she yelled at him. 'I just like watching television! I like nature programmes and gardening programmes and slushy old black-and-white films. Is that a crime?' She slammed down the tea plate she had been about to hand to Alex, so hard that it broke in half down the middle. She didn't seem to care as she picked up another plate and looked like she might slam that down at any minute too. She told him that he had no right to force his own views on everybody else and that television was a godsend for many people like herself who needed it for company. As she said all this, her voice got louder and her face got pinker and Mr Rutherford didn't say a word.

Finally, when she'd finished, he waited for a few moments before responding. 'I wish you'd told me how you felt, Mrs Daniels. I have no wish to deprive you of something which is obviously so important to you.' And he did look genuinely sorry to hear that he had done that – or at least *would* have done, if she hadn't still been watching all her programmes up in the tower room in any case.

Mrs Daniels looked taken aback. 'You don't?'

'Of course not! If you want a television in your own room then that's fine with me,' Mr Rutherford continued.

'So, Dad,' Alex put in quickly, 'does this mean you don't want to deprive *me* of TV any longer either?'

His father gave him a sympathetic smile as if he

admired Alex for trying, then shook his head. 'I think being deprived of television, at least for a little while, is good for your development. Mrs Daniels has already developed, so that's why it doesn't apply to her.'

Alex scowled. 'That's rubbish!'

Mr Rutherford laughed, but in a warm rather than a dismissive sort of way, and I could see that at least he was letting Alex have the last word for once – even though Alex probably wasn't appreciating that right now.

'Well, then . . .' Mrs Daniels began, stiffly, 'since you don't mind, I think I'll go and bring my television down to my sitting room right away. I shall be much more comfortable watching it there. There's another good film starting shortly.'

'Isn't it a bit late to be watching films?' Mr Rutherford asked, glancing up at the kitchen clock.

'Not for me – I've never been a person who needs a lot of sleep. Besides, they're showing *Rebecca*. It's one of my favourites.'

'*Rebecca*?' I blurted out, hardly able to believe it.

Mrs Daniels nodded and gave me a pointed look. 'I rather like the housekeeper in it,' she said.

✻ 21 ✻

One month later I was sitting on the plane that was going to take me to Australia. It had been a difficult decision for Ben, but in the end he had decided to let me have my big adventure.

It was the beginning of September and Ben wanted me to go now before the school term started here, even though he wasn't starting university until October. He'd succeeded in getting a place at a university that was less than two hours away from Thornton Hall on the train, which meant he was going to travel back some weekends to work in the garden. He was going to move up into the main house after I'd gone and apparently, when I returned from Australia, I would be able to live there too, until Ben finished university and we could afford a place of our own again. I was only going to be gone for a year. Then Louise and Greg and I would all be coming home to England together – at least, that was the plan. (I ought to mention that I'd been feeling a lot friendlier towards Greg since he'd offered to help Lou pay for my ticket to Australia.)

Ben was excited about studying history and getting to be a student like he'd always wanted, but he also said that he would really miss me. I told him that I felt the same. I was excited about going to Australia and seeing Louise again, but I was also worried that I would really miss Ben while I was there.

An hour earlier, as we'd waited together at the airport for a member of the airline staff to come and collect me, I had told Ben that I was starting to feel scared. I was worried about the long journey I was going to have to make all alone – especially as I'd never flown before. And something else was worrying me too.

'You're not cross with me for not staying here with you, are you?' I asked him.

Ben shook his head. 'It was my decision to let you go. Why would I be cross?'

'But . . . you know . . . are you cross with me for *wanting* to go?'

'Of course not! Look, this is a really good opportunity for you. I can see why you want to go! And what we both have to remember is that we're not *losing* each other. It's not like that, OK?'

I nodded, trying to think positively like Louise had always taught me to do and like Ben was always struggling to do.

There was something else I was frightened of – something I was sure *would* make Ben angry if I told him about it now, just as I was about to step on to the plane. But somehow I couldn't hold back from blurting it out. 'What if I don't like it when I get there, Ben?' I could feel tears welling up in my eyes as I added, 'What if I should have stayed at Thornton Hall?'

At Thornton Hall everything was safe and familiar, and Ben wouldn't be very far away.

My brother looked sympathetic as he answered me, but his voice was firm. 'Life *can't* be an adventure if you don't take a few risks, May. Moving to Thornton Hall was a risk too, remember. It's only now that it feels like a really safe place to be.'

It was the sort of answer I'd have expected from Louise, not Ben. Ben was preparing me as best he could for my journey out into the big wide world without him, I could see that. But half of me didn't want him to. Half of me just wanted him to hang on to me and tell me I wasn't allowed to go after all.

As I sat on the plane waiting for it to take off, I really wished that I had Ben sitting beside me. Or Louise. Or even Alex. There was an old lady, but she was wearing an eye-mask and she sounded as if she was having to concentrate especially hard on her breathing.

I suddenly remembered something. Alex and I had given each other presents (as well as exchanging email addresses) when we'd said goodbye. I had given him a new sketch pad and a brand new set of pencils from the art shop in town, but he hadn't let me open the gift he had bought for me. Instead he had made me promise to wait until I got on the plane.

'What's in it?' I'd asked, shaking the flat package to see if I could guess. It felt like a book to me.

But he had just grinned and replied, 'One last secret.'

Now that I was sitting on board with my seat belt fastened, I took the present out of my bag and started to unwrap it, pretty certain that I already knew what it was. I was sure that Alex had given me

the book of *The Secret Garden*. I still hadn't got round
to reading the actual book yet, though in a funny way
I no longer felt I needed to, now that Mary Lennox
and I had sort of gone our separate ways. I liked to
think of Mary after the story finishes, growing up in
her big house with all her new friends and her garden
that didn't have to be a secret one any longer. And
my story was continuing just as happily, I thought
now – happily, but differently.

So I got a surprise when I undid the wrapping.
Inside was a notebook with a yellow rose on the front,
and when I flicked it open I saw that Alex had written inside the front cover: *This is so you can keep a diary
of all your adventures – I reckon you'll have lots of time to
start writing it while you're on the plane!*

'It's Mary, isn't it?' An air hostess was bending
down over me to introduce herself. As she checked to
see that my seat belt was fastened properly she
asked, 'Is everything all right?'

I nodded. 'But everyone calls me *May*,' I said.

'What a lovely name!'

'Yes,' I agreed, smiling because May was suddenly
the name that made me feel most *real*.

'Well, is there anything I can get for you, May?'

I started to shake my head, then stopped as I
thought of something. 'Have you got a pen, please?'
I asked her.

She gave me one and I settled back in my seat and
opened the notebook Alex had given me. Inside – on
the page opposite Alex's message – I wrote my name
and the date. Then I began to write down everything
I could remember about what had happened this
summer so that I'd never forget it. It was going to
take me a while, but I had plenty of time. There were

loads of pages in my new diary, which was lucky, because I knew I needed to leave plenty of space for all the exciting things that were going to happen to me in Australia.

The videos and DVDs that May talks about in *The Making of May* are based on real books.

The Secret Garden is by Frances Hodgson Burnett and published by Puffin Books.

Rebecca and *Jane Eyre* are really for older readers, but you might enjoy them.

Rebecca is by Daphne du Maurier and published by Virago Press.

Jane Eyre is by Charlotte Brontë and published by Penguin Books.

Also by Gwyneth Rees

The Mum Hunt

Matthew pulled a scornful face. 'How can you miss someone you've never known?'

Esmie does miss her mum, even though she was only a tiny baby when she died. She has a photo by her bed – and sometimes, when she needs advice or just fancies a chat, she asks her mum for help. Sometimes she even hears her reply.

But Esmie thinks her dad is lonely. And her big brother, Matthew, would definitely benefit from a female influence. So Esmie decides to take action – she's going to find her dad a girlfriend. Beautiful, clever, charming, kind to children and animals . . . How hard can it be to find the perfect partner for your dad?

Winner of the Younger Novel category of the Red House Children's Book Award 2004

Also by Gwyneth Rees

The Mum Detective

'You'd make a really good mum detective,' Holly said. 'One who specializes in finding missing mothers.'

Esmie is really excited that her dad is getting on so well with Lizzie, his new girlfriend. Lizzie is so nice Esmie sometimes even forgets about her real mother, who died when she was a baby.

But then Lizzie starts behaving strangely – saying she's at work when she's not. Esmie plotted for so long to bring her dad and Lizzie together. Could she be about to lose her second mum – before she's even got to know her?

A selected list of titles available from Macmillan Children's Books

The prices shown below are correct at the time of going to press. However, Macmillan Publishers reserves the right to show new retail prices on covers, which may differ from those previously advertised.